In Memory Of ...

Nicole Devitt

2006

12/06

CHRISTMAS
IN MY HEART

15

FOCUS ON THE FAMILY®

CHRISTMAS IN MY HEART

A TREASURY OF TIMELESS
CHRISTMAS STORIES

15

compiled and edited by
JOE L. WHEELER

TYNDALE HOUSE PUBLISHERS, INC., CAROL STREAM, ILLINOIS

Visit Tyndale's exciting Web site at www.tyndale.com

Visit Joe Wheeler's Web site at www.joewheelerbooks.com

TYNDALE and Tyndale's quill logo are registered trademarks of Tyndale House Publishers, Inc.

Focus on the Family is a registered trademark of Focus on the Family, Colorado Springs, Colorado.

Christmas in My Heart is a registered trademark of Joe L. Wheeler and may not be used by anyone else in any form.

Christmas in My Heart 15

Woodcut illustrations are from the library of Joe L. Wheeler.

Designed by Jennifer Ghionzoli

Edited by Kimberly Miller

Series designed by Jenny Swanson

Published in association with WordServe Literary Group, Ltd., 10152 Knoll Circle, Highlands Ranch, CO 80130.

Library of Congress Cataloging-in-Publication Data

Christmas in my heart / [compiled by] Joe L. Wheeler.
   p. cm.
   ISBN-13: 978-1-4143-0136-5 (15)
   ISBN-10: 1-4143-0136-7 (15)
   1. Christmas stories, American.   I. Wheeler, Joe L., date
PS648.C45C447   1992
813'.01833—dc20

Printed in the United States of America

12   11   10   09   08   07   06
7   6   5   4   3   2   1

DEDICATION

Way back with *Christmas in My Heart 1* and *2*, it happened. I received a letter from a Canadian housewife, mother, and author. She'd fallen in love with the two books—and had both questions and observations. I responded, and so it began.

Through the years, she has gradually become one of our most cherished friends.

Most of the Canadian Christmas stories we've anthologized through the years have been unearthed by her. Case in point: She submitted "A Christmas Bargain in Kisses," found in this collection.

Unquestionably, however, the most valuable contribution she's made has been as one of the four editors who read and critique each story I write before it is submitted for publication. So seriously does she take that pro bono responsibility that sometimes the text is slashed to pieces before it's tossed back into my lap. But given that her suggested edits are so insightful, invariably the story is greatly improved as a result.

A couple of years ago, I sent her a story I had written hurriedly, as I was rushing about getting ready for a cruise. Once on the high seas, I blissfully relaxed. But there was no escape from her, even there! A blistering e-mail reached me, declaring, in so many words, "How DARE you even think of submitting a story that is unworthy of you? How dare you let all those readers down who've come to expect only the very best from you!" So chastened was I that, upon my return,

I completely abandoned the poor brainchild and wrote, in its stead, one of my longest stories, "Christmas after the Dark Time," for Tyndale/Focus on the Family and the much shorter "Road Closed Ahead" for Review and Herald.

So it is indeed fitting that I dedicate *Christmas in My Heart 15* to

LINDA HARRINGTON STEINKE

of

Warburg, Alberta

CONTENTS

ACKNOWLEDGMENTS

"Give or Take," (Introduction) by Joseph Leininger Wheeler. Copyright © 2005. Printed by permission of the author.

"If You're Missing Baby Jesus, Call 7162," by Jean Gietzen. Published in *Virtue*, December 1983. Reprinted by permission of the author.

"Eric's Gift," by Deborah Smoot, published in *Plus Magazine*, December 1989. Reprinted by permission of the author.

"Forty Dollars to Spend," by Shirley Seifert. Published in *McCall's*, January 1930. If anyone can provide knowledge of the earliest publication source of this old story, or the whereabouts of the author's next of kin, please send to Joe Wheeler (P.O. Box 1246, Conifer, Colorado 80433).

"The Christmas Pageant," by Michael L. Lindvall. Published in Lindvall's *The Good News from North Haven* (New York: Crossroad Publishing, 2002). Republished by permission of Copyright Clearance Center.

"The House That Glowed," by Arthur Maxwell. Published in volume 7 of *Uncle Arthur's Bedtime Stories* (Hagerstown, MD: Review and Herald Publishing, 1964). Reprinted by permission of Malcolm Maxwell and Review and Herald Publishing.

"Please, Sir, I Want to Buy a Miracle," as retold by Albert P. Stauderman. If anyone can provide knowledge of the earliest publication source of this old story or the whereabouts of the author's next of kin, please send to Joe Wheeler (P.O. Box 1246, Conifer, Colorado 80433).

"O Little Flock," by Temple Bailey. If anyone can provide knowledge of the earliest publication source of this old story or the whereabouts of the author's next of kin, please send to Joe Wheeler (P.O. Box 1246, Conifer, Colorado 80433).

"A Christmas Bargain in Kisses," author unknown. Published in *The Nor-West Farmer*, during 1900–1902. Text owned by Joe Wheeler (P.O. Box 12146, Conifer, Colorado 80433).

"The Secretary of the Treasury Plays Santa Claus," by Sara L. Guerin. Published in *St. Nicholas*, January 1894. Text owned by Joe Wheeler (P.O. Box 1246, Conifer, Colorado 80433).

Joseph Leininger Wheeler

INTRODUCTION:
GIVE OR TAKE

Socrates knew it thousands of years ago: the "sure thing" may not be.

We're slow learners: We still don't know it.

❋ ❋ ❋

*T*t is 105 degrees in the shade, and the summer sun wilts me as I stand outside a house, gratefully lowering my briefcase to the porch floor. Since that briefcase weighs well over forty pounds, I seem to walk with a permanent stoop.

Finally, after I knock loudly, the inner door opens—a little. The screen door does not. The lady of the house peers out at me with the coldest eyes this side of the North Pole, suspecting that I'm there with the deliberate intention of separating her from the little household money she's managed to put aside.

Which I am.

She listens impassively while I give my shopworn spiel, and all the while she slowly and almost imperceptibly begins to close the door. Clearly, I have about as much chance of getting inside and showing her the books in my battered briefcase as I'd have selling refrigerators to Eskimos during a blizzard.

In my despair, I play my trump card. "Ma'am, could I ask a big favor of you?"

In surprise she freezes: The door ceases to close, and she spits out a malevolent, *"What?!"* If I were to expand on that single-word retort it would be this: *I'm in the process of shutting my door on you, so whatever it is that you're going to ask me is going to result in one single thing: This door is going to close, the lock will be set from inside, you will leave, and my meager supply of money will remain intact.*

Whatever it is that she imagines the favor might be, she's totally unprepared for the question.

I manage to look woebegone, exhausted, and overcome by the blinding sun (easy, considering the conditions). I smile weakly and say, "It's *so* hot today, would it be too much trouble if I asked you for a glass of water? . . . I'll pay you back when it rains."

Miracle. The door opens again, her lips twitch, and suddenly I'm no longer an enemy, but instead a rather nice-looking young college student standing out there in the blistering heat. She says, "You *poor* kid—must be hot out there! Would you prefer a nice glass of cold lemonade?"

She leaves, and I hear a cupboard door closing, and then a refrigerator door. Soon she returns, glass in hand and a smile on her face. She has to open the screen door to hand me the drink. And I am prepared. I say, "Bless you, ma'am! . . .While I'm drinking it, you might be interested in something I've been lugging around in this monstrosity of a briefcase." I hand her a Bible storybook . . . and take my time drinking.

The attitude of the woman has now shifted 180 degrees. I'm no longer her enemy but rather her *guest*. Which translates internally to, *I'm the hostess, and I've always believed in hospitality. This kid seems nice, and the longer I leave this front door open, the hotter the house is going to get.* "Come on in! Take a seat. I see you need a refill."

And the sale is already two-thirds made.

For five summers, I used this last-resort approach to salvage situations that were otherwise doomed to failure. Again and again, I saw it work. Even if the woman regretfully had to tell me she couldn't afford the books, that her husband had lost his job, and that her kids desperately needed clothes before books, when I left the house, I had become in that short time someone she really liked, enjoyed talking to, and hoped to see again!

And when she waved good-bye, it was as a hostess might bid adieu to a beloved guest.

As for me, I truly appreciated that glass of lemonade—not only because it quenched my thirst but also because it connected me to my potential customer.

Not all gift recipients, however, are quite so grateful. Most of us labor under the delusion that if we only shower people with enough goodies and gifts, they'll love us for life and ever afterward think of us fondly.

Not so. Of giving, Emerson said, "We do not quite forgive the giver. The hand that feeds us is in some danger of being bitten."

❄ ❄ ❄

So what could this have to do with Christmas?

A lot.

Let's apply it to gift giving at Christmastime. Most people I know spend a great deal of thought to carefully select gifts that they hope will delight their families and friends. Yet after reading thousands of Christmas stories, I have come to realize—especially from the true stories—that the most fondly remembered Christmases usually involved self-sacrifice on the part of the person doing the remembering.

Again and again in real life, I've seen parents pay a heavy price for showering their children with things without offsetting these gifts by encouraging their children to develop a selfless spirit of giving to others. The result is lifelong selfishness, egocentricity, and the tragic mind-set of one who thinks, *The world owes me a living.* And tragically, parents who martyr themselves so that their children may have anything they ask for almost invariably are trampled upon in later life by their ungrateful grown children.

Almost all of us are born selfish; consequently true generosity is an acquired trait. It is taught by wise parents or other mentors, circumstances, or example, rarely by abstract lectures or sermons.

In retrospect, for most of us, the epiphany that changes the course of our lives occurs when someone— usually a parent—almost forces us to substitute the needs of others for our own yearnings and desires, and our lives are never the same again. For selfless giving (giving in secret without recognition, reward, or payback) is the ultimate type of giving associated with our Lord. Again and again in His earthly ministry, Jesus urged His listeners not only to give sacrificially, but also anonymously. And because the post-apostolic bishop St. Nicholas did just that, we still fondly remember him seventeen centuries after he lived.

Yet the window of opportunity to dramatically change the lives of our children for the better in this respect is open such a *short* time. In the almost frantic pace of babyhood, childhood, and adolescence, parents frequently discover too late that their children have left them and are now mentored by others. The God-entrusted opportunity and obligation is now gone forever, the tree already being bent.

I wish I could say that I have so learned this lesson that I practice it with our grandchildren. Instead I sense that our daughter and son-in-law have to do damage control from the gifts we shower upon their two sons. Two years ago, both sets of grandparents were together under one roof, and we seemed determined to outshower the other!

There too, we must learn to practice what we preach. Perhaps as grandparents *we* need to assist in this life-changing process and help, rather than hinder, in terms of lighting the spark that may flame into lifelong selfless generosity in these beloved grandchildren.

There is, after all, nothing wrong in our giving, though both our motives and attitude count a great deal. But there *is* something gravely wrong when children are permitted to grow up ungrateful and devoid of a belief structure that makes selfless giving one of their greatest joys. By selfless giving, I mean giving without recognition or expectation of gifts of equal value being given in return—the hardest type of giving there is. For we are all born to selfishness and a terminal case of you-can't-thank-me-enough-ishness. And the only power in the universe strong enough to shatter that core of selfishness is God.

SO THIS CHRISTMAS . . .

Let us determine that it will be different in that respect, that we will tackle that most daunting challenge of all and in the midst of affluence, nurture the spirit of true generosity in our families. Interestingly enough, in less-privileged countries I've lived in or visited, I have noticed a disproportionate love of giving and contentedness with life in general, compared to the greed and dissatisfaction so prevalent in our own country and in other affluent nations.

So let us deliberately plan activities and projects for our children that will enable them, perhaps for the first time, to move beyond themselves and catch a glimpse of lifelong service for others. As vehicles of discussion in such a life-changing attitudinal shift, I invite you to read stories in this collection that have to do with such giving: "Eric's Gift," "If You're Missing Baby Jesus, Call 7162," "Carla's Gift," "Miracle at Midnight," "O Little Flock," "Forty Dollars to Spend," "The House That Glowed," "The Wheelchair," "Please, Sir, I Want to Buy a Miracle," "The Secretary of the Treasury Plays Santa Claus," and "The Forgotten Santa."

And we'd be honored if you'd let us know the results.

CODA

I look forward to hearing from you! Please do keep the stories, responses, and suggestions coming—and not just for Christmas stories. I am putting together collections centered on other genres as well. You may reach me by writing to:

Joe L. Wheeler, PhD
P.O. Box 1246
Conifer, CO 80433

May the Lord bless and guide the ministry of these stories in your home.

Jean Gietzen

IF YOU'RE MISSING BABY JESUS, CALL 7162

World War II was raging, and Christmas had come again. Somewhere in the family's moves, their nativity set had been lost. So they bought another.

Only trouble was: There were two figurines of the baby Jesus. So what to do?

❄ ❄ ❄

So many people have urged us to include this that it is easily the write-in story of the year!

❄ ❄ ❄

*I*n the depths of a bitterly cold December, my mother decided it simply wouldn't do to go through the holidays without a nativity set.

It was 1943 in a small town in North Dakota. My father worked for an oil company during my growing-up years, and we moved around to several different parts of the state with his job. At some point between one move and another, we lost our family's little manger scene.

Happily, Mother found another at our local five-and-dime for only $3.99. When my brother and I helped her unpack the set, however, we found two figurines of the baby Jesus.

Mother frowned. "Someone must have packed this wrong," she said, counting out the pieces. "We have one Joseph, one Mary, three wise men, three shepherds, two lambs, a donkey, a cow, an angel—and two babies. Oh dear! I suppose some set down at the store is missing a baby Jesus."

"Hey, that's great, Mom," my brother said with a laugh. "Now we have twins!"

Mother wouldn't have a bit of it. "You two run right back down to the store and tell the manager that we have an extra Jesus."

"Ah, Mom."

"Go on with you now. Tell him to put a sign on the remaining boxes saying that if a set is missing a baby Jesus, call 7162."

She smiled. "I'll give you each a penny for some candy. And don't forget your mufflers. It's freezing cold out there."

The manager copied down my mother's message, and

sure enough, the next time we were in the store we saw his cardboard sign:

"If you're missing baby Jesus, call 7162."

All week long we waited for the call to come. *Surely,* we thought, *someone was missing that important figurine.*

What was a nativity set without the main attraction? Each time the phone rang, my mother would say, "I'll bet that's about Jesus."

But it never was.

With increasing exasperation, my father tried to explain that the figurine could be missing from a set anywhere—Minot, Fargo, or even Walla Walla, Washington, for that matter. After all, packing errors occurred all the time. He suggested we just put the extra Jesus back in the box and forget about it.

"Back in the box!!" I wailed. "What a terrible thing to do to the baby Jesus. And at Christmas, too."

"Someone will surely call," my mother reasoned. "We'll just keep the babies together in the manger until we find the owner."

That made my brother and me happy. It was special to look into that little manger and see two Christ children, side by side, gazing up into the adoring eyes of Mary. And was that a surprised look on Joseph's face?

But the days went by, and no one called. When we still hadn't heard from anyone by five o'clock on Christmas Eve, my mother insisted that Daddy "just run down to the store" to see if there were any sets left.

"You can see them right through the window, over the counter," she said. "If they're all gone, I'll know someone is bound to call tonight."

"Run down to the store?" my father thundered. "Ethel, it's fifteen below zero out there!"

"Oh, Daddy," I said, "we'll go with you. Won't we, Tommy?" Tommy nodded vigorously. "We'll bundle up good. And . . . we can look at all the decorations on the way."

My father blew out a long sigh and headed for the front closet. "I can't believe I'm doing this," he muttered. "Every time the phone rings everybody yells at me to see if it's about Jesus. And now I'm going off on the coldest night of the year to peek in some store window to see if He's there or not there."

Daddy muttered all the way down the block in the cold, still air, while my brother and I raced each other to the store. The streets were empty and silent. But behind each lighted window, we knew that families were gathering around Christmas trees and manger scenes and fireplaces and tables laden with tasty holiday treats.

I was the first to reach the store window, where colored lights flickered along the edge of the frosty pane. Pushing my nose up against the glass, I peered into the darkened store.

"They're all gone, Daddy!" I yelled. "Every set must be sold."

"Hooray!" my brother cheered, catching up with me. "The mystery will be solved tonight!"

My father, who had seen no logical reason to run, remained some yards behind us. When he heard our tidings, he turned on his heel and started for home.

Inside the house once more, we were surprised to see only one baby Jesus in the manger. Where was the twin? For that matter, where was Mother? Had she vanished, too?

Daddy was unperturbed. "Someone must have called," he reasoned, pulling off his boots. "She must have gone out to deliver the figurine. You kids get busy stringing those popcorn strands for the tree, and I'll wrap your mother's present."

We had almost completed one strand when the phone rang. "You get it, Jean," my father called. "Tell 'em we already found a home for Jesus!"

My brother gave me a quick, eager look. Our mystery would be solved at last.

But the telephone call didn't solve any mystery at all. It created a much bigger one.

It was my mother on the phone, with instructions for us to come to 205 Chestnut Street immediately, and to bring three blankets, a box of cookies, and some milk.

My father was incredulous. "I can't believe this," he groaned, retrieving his boots for the second time that evening. "*Now* what has she gotten us into?" He paused. "205 Chestnut. Why, that's eight blocks away. Wrap that milk up good in the blankets or it'll turn to ice by the time we get there. Why can't we just get on with Christmas? It's probably twenty below out there now. And the wind's pickin' up. Of all the crazy things to do on a night like this."

Tommy and I didn't mind at all. It was Christmas Eve, and we were in the middle of an adventure. We sang carols at the top of our lungs all the way to Chestnut Street. My father, carrying his bundle of blankets, milk, and cookies, looked for all of the world like St. Nicholas with his arms full of goodies.

My brother called back to him. "Hey, Dad, let's pretend we're looking for a place to stay—just like Joseph 'n' Mary."

"Let's pretend we're in Bethlehem where it's probably sixty-five degrees in the shade right now," my father answered.

The house at 205 Chestnut turned out to be the darkest one on the block. One tiny light burned in the living room, and the moment we set foot on the front porch steps my mother opened the door and shouted, "They're here, they're here! Oh, thank goodness you got here, Ray! You kids take those blankets into the living room and wrap up the little ones on the couch. I'll take the milk and cookies."

"Ethel, would you mind telling me what's going on here?" my father huffed. "We've just hiked through sub-zero weather with the wind in our faces all the way—"

"Never mind all that now," my mother interrupted. "There's no heat in this house, and this young mother doesn't know what to do. Her husband walked out on her. Those poor little children will have a very bleak Christmas, so don't you complain. I told her you could fix that oil furnace in a jiffy."

Well, that stopped my father right in his tracks.

My mother strode off to the kitchen to warm the milk, while my brother and I wrapped up the five little children who huddled together on the couch. The distraught young mother, wringing her hands, explained to my father that her husband had run off, taking bedding, clothing, and almost every piece of furniture. But she'd been doing all right, she explained, until the furnace broke down.

"I've been doing washin' and ironin' for folks, and cleanin' the five-n-dime," she said. "I—I saw your number every day there, on those boxes on the counter. Then—when the furnace went out—that number kept goin' through my mind. 7162. 7162.

"Said on the box that if a person was missin' Jesus, they should call you. That's how I knew you was good Christian people, willin' to help folks. I figured that maybe you'd help me, too. So I stopped at the grocery store tonight and called your missus. I'm not missin' Jesus, Mister, because I surely love the Lord. But I am missin' heat.

"Me and the kids ain't got no beddin' and no warm clothes. I got a few Christmas toys for 'em, but I got no money to fix that furnace."

"It's okay," my father said gently. "You called the right number. Now, let's see here. You've got a little oil burner there in the dining room. Shouldn't be too hard to fix. Probably just a clogged flue. I'll look it over; see what it needs."

My mother came into the living room carrying a plate of cookies and a tray of cups with warm milk. As she set the cups down on the coffee table, I noticed the figure of the baby Jesus—our twin—lying in the center of the table. There was no Mary or Joseph, no wise men or shepherds. Just Jesus.

The children stared wide-eyed with wonder at the plate of cookies my mother set before them. One of the littlest ones woke up and crawled out from under the blanket. Seeing all the strangers in his house, his face puckered up, and he began to cry. My mother swooped him in her arms and began to sing to him.

This, this, is Christ the King
Whom shepherds guard and angels sing . . .

Mother crooned, while the child wailed.

Haste, haste, to bring Him laud,
the Babe, the son of Mary.

She went on singing, oblivious to the child's cries.
She danced the baby around the room until finally, in
spite of himself, he settled down again.

"You hear that, Chester?" the young woman said to
another child. "That nice lady is singin' 'bout the Lord
Jesus. He ain't ever gonna walk out on us. Why, He
sent these people to us just to fix our furnace. And blankets—now we got blankets, too! Oh, we'll be warm
tonight. Jesus saves, that's what He does."

My father, finishing his work on the oil burner,
wiped his hands on his muffler. "I've got it goin',
ma'am, but you need more oil. I'll make a few calls
tonight when I get home and we'll get you some.

"Yessir," he said with a sudden smile. "You called the
right number."

When Daddy figured the furnace was going strong
once more, our family bundled up and made our way
home under a clear, starry heaven. My father didn't say
a thing about the cold weather. I could tell he was turning things around in his mind all the way home. As
soon as we set foot inside the front door, he strode over
to the telephone and dialed a number.

"Ed? This is Ray. How are ya? Yes, Merry Christmas
to you, too. Say, Ed, we have kind of an unusual situa-

tion here tonight. I know you've got that pickup truck, and I was wonderin' if we could round up some of the boys and find a Christmas tree, you know, and a couple things for . . ."

The rest of the conversation was lost in a blur as my brother and I ran to our rooms and began pulling clothes out of our closets and toys off our shelves.

My mother checked through our belongings for sizes and selected some of the games she said "might do." Then she added some of her own sweaters and slacks to our stack.

It was a Christmas Eve like no other.

Instead of going to bed in a snug, warm house, dreaming of a pile of presents to open on Christmas morning, we were up way past our bedtime, wrapping gifts for a little family we'd only just met. The men my father had called found oil for the furnace, bedding, two chairs, and three lamps. They made two trips to 205 Chestnut before the night was done.

On the second trip, he let us go, too. Even though it must have been thirty below by then, my father let us ride in the back of the truck, with our gifts stacked all around us.

My brother's eyes danced in the starlight. Without saying anything, we both knew Christmas could never be the same after this. The extra Jesus in our home hadn't been ours to keep after all. He was for someone else . . . for a desperate family in a dark little house on Chestnut Street.

Someone who needed Jesus as much as we did.

And we got to take Him there.

Jean Gietzen

Jean Gietzen continues to write from her home in Milwaukee, Wisconsin.

Deborah Smoot

ERIC'S GIFT

Why was it, the teacher thought with a groan, that the children did well on all the Christmas carols—all but one.

If only Eric would sing the right words. . . .

❄ ❄ ❄

*C*ome, they told me, dum-ditty-dum-dum. . . ."
I stopped the chorus of four-year-olds midstream
in the song and looked *directly* at Eric.

"Eric, this song is called 'The Little Drummer Boy,'"
I spoke sternly, "and the words are 'Come, they told
me, pa-rum-pum-pum-pum,' not 'dum-ditty-dum-
dum.' And, Eric, you don't need to yell. We can hear
you above everyone else. Just sing, Eric. You know,
sing!"

"Eric, Eric, Eric," I muttered under my breath as
I walked back to the music stand.

Eric had two speeds: on and off. I never saw off.
I imagined "off" happened for Eric sometime between
1 and 3 a.m. This shiny-faced wisp of a boy had more
energy than any child I had ever met. He simply could
not hold still. He shifted; he twitched; he giggled; he
yawned; and when he sang, he yelled.

He smelled of soap and Brylcreem, and of clothes that
had been hung out on the line to dry. Two yellow-
striped T-shirts, faded and frayed at the neck, one pair
of black Levi's, and a red hooded sweatshirt constituted
his entire school wardrobe. But his clothes were always
clean and pressed. Mornings at our public preschool
always found Eric scrubbed and polished, and ready for
action. He was obviously loved.

And, I must admit, there was much about Eric that
was lovable. Through all his perpetual motion, he
smiled. In fact, he never quit smiling. His face carried a
nonstop, tooth-filled grin. And when Eric's grin caught
you head-on, it was impossible to stay mad at him.

Three times a week, on the front row of the
preschool chorus, Eric stood grinning and yelling;

although in all fairness to him, he thought he was singing! It's just that Eric loved to sing, and he belted out those Christmas songs as though his life depended on it. He raised the roof, if not our spirits.

There were, however, a couple of problems with that. One, Eric was one of eight children bused from the other side of town. His enthusiasm alone made him the uncontested "star" of the chorus. Some of the mothers were upset that one of those "other" children was stealing the show. Two, Eric could never remember the words. Because his enthusiasm made him a natural leader, soon the whole chorus was singing, "Come, they told me, dum-ditty-dum-dum" and then pealing off into uncontrolled laughter.

I was trying to work on both problems. I sent the words of the song home with Eric to memorize. And some of the mothers were making stiff, white collars with big red bows so this chorus of middle-class children sprinkled with the "ragtag bunch" (as one mother called them) would look unified, even if they didn't sound it!

❄ ❄ ❄

The final rehearsal went well until we got to "The Little Drummer Boy."

"Come they told me," was followed by hesitation, then silence. The piano went on with the melody, but the four-year-olds were so confused with *hum* and *dum* and *pum* that they simply froze. Except for Eric. "Dum-ditty-dum-dum," he finished the phrase.

"That's it!" I screamed and stopped the chorus. "We

are not singing about the seven dwarfs! This is a Christmas song, a *special* song about a little boy just like you—except that he lived long ago when baby Jesus was born. He was poor, but he wanted more than anything to visit the newborn baby in the manger. When he got there, he saw kings and wise men waiting to see baby Jesus. They all had expensive gifts to give the Christ child—things like gold and jewels and perfume. Well, when the boy saw all those fancy people with all their expensive gifts, he just about turned around and went home. I mean, he was just a kid with nothing to give. About the only thing he could do was play his drum.

"But then he looked around and realized that baby Jesus, too, was poor, that He was born in a stable. (That's like a barn where they kept the animals.) So, when it was the boy's turn to see Jesus, he asked if he could play his drum for the baby, and Mary said yes. Well, everyone loved it, and the boy learned that the best gift you can give is the gift of yourself!"

I finished the story and, satisfied that the children understood it, went on: "When we sing the song, we are making the sound of the little boy's drum. It is a *p* sound. Everybody say it with me: 'pa, pa, pum.' Now everyone say 'pum' twenty times."

✳ ✳ ✳

While the preschool chorus repeated the words, I looked at the clock. I had taken too long telling the story of the little drummer boy. Our rehearsal time was gone.

"Okay, children," I finished up, "there is no more time to practice, but you have to remember the drum makes a *p* sound." They ran off to lunch, "pumming" all the way.

I walked back to their classroom teacher, who was sitting on a chair at the rear of the auditorium watching the rehearsal. Discouraged, I sat down beside her. "Tell me about Eric," I requested.

"Well, there isn't much to tell," she said. "As far as we know, he is an only child being raised by his grandmother. We've never met her. Eric told us she didn't want to come to Back to School Night because she was afraid someone would find out she can't read. Apparently, his grandmother is an illiterate woman who stands in the shadows and, as best she can on a welfare check, loves and cares for her little boy." The teacher stood up. "I'd better check on the children," she finished. "Good luck, Debbie."

I went to the office to look up Eric's records. He lived alone with his paternal grandmother. There was an address, but no phone number. I wrote a special note inviting her to the program and sent it home with Eric—pinned to his shirt so she would be sure to see it. Surely, if his grandmother couldn't read the note, she knew someone who could read it to her.

The day of the Christmas program arrived. The parents came armed with cameras and video recorders. I stood in the hall with the preschool chorus. Eric had on a new white dress shirt that he wanted to show me. He was higher than a kite. The whole chorus was excited, wiggling even more than usual. The stiff white collars were driving them crazy. I barked out some last-minute instructions: "You are not to touch those collars

while you are singing, even if you are itching to death!"
That said, we all marched onto the stage.

❊ ❊ ❊

Without a hitch, the children went through the songs:
"Jingle Bells," "Silent Night," "Away in a Manger."
This little crew looked and sounded, for all the world,
like a chorus of angels. It's amazing what white collars
and a touch of the Christmas spirit can do.

I turned the music on the stand to "The Little Drummer Boy," signaled the pianist to begin, and made the
pum sound with my lips to the children as the introduction was playing.

"Come, they told me . . ." they started right on cue.
"Pum-ditty-pum-pum . . ." They hesitated for a
moment before joining Eric. There was no stopping
them now. "I am a poor boy, too. . . ." Eric's voice
soared above the others: "Pum-ditty-pum-pum." *How
could he have forgotten the "pa-rum-pum-pum" part when
I talked to them about it just yesterday?* I could hear the
audience snickering. "Mary nodded . . . pum-ditty-
pum-pum . . ." By now, only about three children were
singing with Eric. The noise from the audience had
scared the others. *What was I thinking? This song is way
too hard for a group of four-year-olds.*

The children were frozen and embarrassed, and so
was I. We all wanted to crawl off stage, all except for
Eric. "The ox and lamb kept time," he yelled, "pum-
ditty-pum-pum." And he grinned and continued.
"I played my drum for Him, pum-ditty-pum-pum." By
now, Eric was singing a solo, "I played my best for

Him." He didn't even seem to notice that no one else was singing. "Pum-ditty-pum-pum-ditty-pum-pum. . . ."

Eric's "pum-dittys" were bouncing all around the auditorium. The laughter in the audience was now uncontrollable. Finally, and I mean *finally*, the song ended, and a bunch of bewildered four-year-olds bowed and got off the stage as fast as possible, totally out of order.

Before I could get out of the school, the hallway filled with parents and children in white collars. Leading the pack was Eric, pulling a short, gray-haired woman by the hand.

Eric made a beeline for me. "Mrs. Smoot, this is my grandma." He dragged her up to my side and grinned. "She rode the bus all the way here to see the program." He was obviously pleased that she had made the trip. "She wants to tell you thanks!" he yelled.

I turned to his grandmother and started to speak.

"Well, I'm happy to meet you," I said. "Eric is . . ." There was a vacant stare in her bright eyes. I noticed large hearing aids in both her ears. She smiled, obviously confused.

"She says she's happy to meet you, too," Eric blurted out. He was acting as a translator for his grandmother, who I now realized was almost totally deaf. "Boy, isn't Christmas great, Mrs. Smoot?" Eric continued. "Sorry I sang so loud, but that song about the little drummer boy is such a great story, I wanted my grandma to hear it!"

Eric's grandmother didn't seem to hear a word we were saying. But standing there silently in a purple-flowered dress, she could see Eric's excitement and his love of the music. She looked at me for a moment, her eyes filled with tears, and spontaneously reached up to hug me. "Thank you," she whispered.

"Thank you," I said back as I looked in her eyes. "Thank you for Eric." I embraced her again.

Tenderly, she then removed Eric's white collar, handed it to me, and took her grandson's hand. I watched them walk down the hall. Eric was bouncing at her side and singing, "Pum-ditty-pum-pum" all the way out the door.

※ ※ ※

I never hear "The Little Drummer Boy" without remembering Eric's gift to his grandmother and her gift of unconditional love for him. I never read the story of that little drummer boy without recalling the miracle in the manger: God's greatest gift of all—His love. I realize that when I sometimes tune Him out, God yells His love to me. And every time I sing this carol, though I don't sing it that way out loud, in my heart the words will always be "pum-ditty-pum-pum."

Deborah Smoot
Deborah Smoot writes today from her home in Park City, Utah.

Shirley Seifert

FORTY DOLLARS TO SPEND

In 1930, forty dollars was a lot of money to Dora
Skipping, having grown up in a manse where there
were always more children, needs, and love than there
was money.

Now she was going home for Christmas. How
should she spend this hard-earned money? Should she
fix up a portion of the threadbare house? She just
didn't know.

And then there was the dilemma of what to do
with Frederick Bain, born to wealth and luxury. He
was to meet her family at Christmas . . . but she

wasn't sure he ought to come. So she telegraphed him,
calling the visit off.

But Father had other ideas.

✻ ✻ ✻

I fell in love with this story eleven Christmases ago,
and each Christmas since it has been a top contender
for a place in Christmas in My Heart. *For some*
strange reason, I just kept saving it. Now I see why:
It was to grace our fifteenth anniversary collection.

✻ ✻ ✻

*T*t was Friday and wash day for Dora Skipping,
because on Friday mornings the other two girls
who shared with her the large room under the northeast
eaves of Rayfield Hall had classes straight through, while
she was free. This washing and renovating of her own
clothes was one of the ways in which she made both
ends of her budget meet. One end of the budget was
simple—a small, small sum of money in the form of a
monthly allowance by mail; the other end was compli-
cated, since she was an extremely pretty girl who had
good taste as well as good looks and ambitions.

Three military cot-beds paraded in a row under the
east windows. On their counterpanes was spread Dora

Skipping's daytime attire—one wool jersey dress, one hand-knitted sweater with a flannel skirt, two frocks of silk crepe. And they were frocks, too, even if Dora *had* made them herself from bargains in material! A mere thing like necessity would never draggle Dora. These costumes, stripped now of their washable accessories, awaited an inspection for spots and a thorough pressing when the laundry should be hung up to dry. The washable accessories, together with a pile of lingerie and her entire supply of silk stockings, were occupying Dora at a stationary porcelain washstand in a small closet-like lavatory.

Dora was working hard and fast. It was no joke, this every-Friday-morning struggle for respectability. With Dora the aim would be even higher. She was a girl at whom people turned to look again, whether she was in sports attire on the campus or at a tea in silk. The handwork on her clothes, the sewing and laundering, were exquisitely done. She always had some duck of a frill here or there, where you least expected it and where you liked it best.

"And I'm clever," she would have explained, laughing, to anybody interested. "I stick to one color. I get most horribly tired of blue, but everything goes together. That's how smart I have to be!" There would be that smile on her lips, and her eyes would dance in an appeal something like this: *Laugh at me all you want so long as you like me.*

You liked her at once, and you thought her clever indeed to choose blue. The faded old blue smock she wore at her washing was distractingly becoming, because her eyes were blue; a very positive blue and not serene or placid, but with the very dickens dancing in their depths. She was so alive, this poor, hardworking girl. Her very hair snapped with vitality. God, who hadn't given her riches, had given her gold-bronze hair that glinted all over with a constant effect of catching a sunbeam, and had supplied odd little curls in the hollow of her white neck and over her ears. Besides these lovely eyes and this enviable hair, Dora Skipping was twenty, healthy, slender, and sweetly rounded of contour; and anybody would suspect in two minutes that somewhere there must be a young man who loved her madly.

✳ ✳ ✳

There was. His name was Frederick Bain, a graduate electrical engineer with an excellent position. He came of people who had means. He drove out to call on Dora or to fetch her elsewhere every weekend. Each time he saw her, the expression on his blunt, honest, not too handsome face was identical. His nice hazel eyes would light up. A stain of red would run under his year-around sunburn and his lips would twitch. He would want to marry Dora Skipping the next minute. Literally the next minute. He said so in every way known to man and some which he thought desperately he had invented.

Finally, the week before this, Dora had admitted that she wanted to marry Fred as much as he wanted to marry her. But it wouldn't be the next minute. It couldn't possibly be one minute before a year from the coming June.

"Gorgeous!" reproached her sweetheart. "How can you be so mean to me?"

"I knew you wouldn't like the idea," sighed Dora. "That's why I waited so long to say yes."

"You knew—a long time ago?" Fred caught his breath sharply.

"Right from the beginning," said Dora appeasingly.

Fred doubled his fists and thrust them into his trousers' pockets. The proposal had been made and accepted this time under trying circumstances. In the afternoon there had been a sleet storm. Roads were treacherous. The dean of women had made an announcement at dinner that no girl was to keep an automobile date that evening. All callers were to be entertained in the parlors of the dormitory. Eight dollars worth of tickets to a show in a city eighteen miles away were going to waste in Fred's pocket this minute. With this entertainment in mind, he had called early. That netted him and Dora an alcove off the main parlor, but there were no curtains to this alcove and right in front of it loomed a piano, played all evening by a brainless male idiot who did things by ear inexhaustibly and kept looking at Dora between times instead of at the girl who had let him in.

"But why a year from June?" protested Fred. "It's wasteful enough to wait at all, but why the extra year—after you've finished school and all?"

"Why do you think you love me?" asked Dora.

"Why do I think—" Fred glared at her helplessly. "Say, if you don't know the answer to that by this time, I'll never be able to tell you."

"I do know," said Dora, so softly that Fred's hands almost ripped through his pockets. "I'm awfully proud and that's why I'm so keen about you. I want everything to be just perfect. I want you to always think a lot of me. If I didn't have a sense of honor, a pretty keen sense of honor, I'd never satisfy a man as honest as you are, I know. But I've a contract to fill—with my family—before I marry anyone."

"What do you mean? A contract?" said poor Fred.

"Have I ever told you about my family?"

"Oh, mentioned them now and then. I know your father is a preacher."

"My father is an angel." Quick tears flashed in Dora's eyes and were winked away. "My father is an angel and my mother is a queen. She came of quite elegant people way south—Georgia. She could have married any number of rich men; I mean, any one of a number. She married Father because she loved him— and he had just nothing. For a long time there was just nothing. Dad was educated to be a lawyer—and the law asked him one time to defend a man who he knew was guilty of a terrible crime, and in his thinking over the ethics of that he turned to the ministry. That was very hard for him and Mother. When I was a little girl we had no carpets on our floors. Dad kept reaching a little more recognition, but there were the babies. We could do without carpets better than without babies, Mother said."

"You sweet kid," said Fred. "You peach! Is it still like that?"

"No, not exactly. Father has a good and loyal church in St. Joseph now. He's quite happy and we're much more comfortable; but when he got to that place, the babies were growing up and had to be educated. You see, that's how we Skippings are. Certain things are awfully

important to us. We're always spending our money on
something highfalutin instead of on carpets. Every
Skipping child had to have a college education. We were
all such prodigies that we must be given a chance to show
the world. No matter how the boys fumed—I had two
older brothers—about pitching in and earning some
luxury, off to school they had to go. John was the first.
He made his own expenses, but that left Father and
Mother with the increasing burden of us and no help.
John was through his first year at a school of architecture
when the war came. He was killed in September of 1918.
None of us older ones can look at the front door at seven
o'clock of a May evening without seeing him standing
there, shouting about some prize he'd taken and that he'd
joined the army."

Fred slid closer on the padded window seat and recklessly laid hold of Dora's hand. Firmly he held it under
the shadow of a too modishly short coattail. Dora blushed
and blinked and laughed with a catch in her throat.

"Then there was James, the brother of John. He got
an appointment to Annapolis. We none of us thought of
anything but how splendid that would be for him. It
was like giving wings to a person who wanted earnestly
to do his duty by all of us but was plainly designed to be
a dashing hero. We made him take the appointment.
His expenses were covered by the government, but now
and then we wanted him to have extras, though it was
hard to make him take them. And the wings came literally. He chose aviation, and we won't let him give that
up. Well, you know how expensive the service is.
About all he can give us, now at any rate, is glory. He's
supposed to marry an heiress; but, being a Skipping, he

won't. He'll marry some priceless gem without a penny—and we'll be so pleased!"

"When are *you* coming?" growled Fred, very fiercely and protectively. He gave every indication of being just about to lose his composure under the politeness of the public parlor.

"I'm next. When I was still small, my grandmother sent Mother's piano from the South. She thought she was doing a kindness, but almost at once it was discovered that I was musical. Then we had music lessons instead of carpets. You couldn't have a much more expensive talent than music. Of course nothing would do but the best teaching, and I couldn't resist because I did love the piano. And the family was so thrilled! We Skippings again! When any one of us is to do something we all forget everything else to get behind that person and push. And so here I am. The head of the music school here is a marvelous pianist, who did concert work until his health broke. He is good; and the idea is that I am getting a touch of college education with my music. So—I finish in June. Yes. But I want a year to pay off a little of my debt. The family doesn't feel that way. I do. You see I haven't been allowed to earn any money except with an occasional accompaniment that Professor Lensing has got me. Practicing four hours a day, I wasn't to think of taking on any jobs. Father has been sending me a monthly allowance, just the same as if he could afford it."

"I see," said Fred, "how you feel, but still—could you make any real money the first year?"

"I would! There's always teaching. For concert practice there's a radio broadcasting station that will give me work once or twice a week, and the organist in Father's church is getting very old. I'd fill in there."

"I'll bet a nickel," said Fred, "I could give you twice as much money to put on that debt and never feel it. I'd be glad to!"

"My dear!" said Dora softly. "I'm sure you would and could, but it wouldn't be the same. I want to give them something all by myself. I want to be one Skipping investment that pays a little."

"Are there more kids?"

"Three." Dora freed her hand suddenly to make a clasping gesture indicating inspiration. "Fred! The holidays begin week after next. Couldn't you come down sometime during Christmas week and meet the Skippings?"

"If I come," said Fred, "I'll bring the largest and most emphatic diamond ring I can buy, and I'll dash their hopes of you entirely. Still inviting me, Dora?"

"I haven't made you know the Skippings at all, goose. When I tell them about you, which I shall at once, if they don't know already, they'll say only, 'How wonderful for Dora!' Gracious, what is all the commotion about?"

Fred shot out his left wrist to look at his watch.

"Ten-twenty," he announced. "At ten-thirty we'll all be booted out the door." He stood before Dora, smiling, coaxing that flattering run of color under his year-around sunburn. "Sweetness," he whispered buzzingly, "won't you come outside to tell me good-bye, or must I wait till a year from June for that?"

The handsome, endowed dormitory opened on a

stone archway through which a miserable wind swirled and whistled; but the only annoyance that at all marred the sweetness of that farewell was the fact that four other couples had got Fred's idea ahead of him. It was all he and Dora could do to find a stone buttress with a shadow suggesting oblivion.

❄ ❄ ❄

So now, on a Friday morning a week later, in the midst of her washing and cleaning, was there any reason in the world why Dora Skipping should think her lot a hard one? When she had hung her wet wash on patent lines above the radiators and turned on the heat full and opened the windows to speed the drying, she unfolded an ironing board and warbled. On a desk before the board she propped a book on harmony and flattered herself that she was doing ear and voice exercise in sight-reading. Strangely, however the harmony exercises began, no matter what the key or the phrasing, Dora Skipping warbled lines from a ballad by De Koven:

Oh, promise me that you will take my hand
The most unworthy in this lowly land.

She had written her family about Fred. They had replied to a man with no time out for argument that they were jubilant at the news and would she, could she possibly have him at home for the holidays or part of the holidays? The Skippings would hold a grand levee, and other precious nonsense of that sort.

Oh, promise me that someday you and I
Will take our love together to some sky—

The Skippings didn't know how grand a levee they would hold when Dora came home—ahead of her Fred, not with him. Oh, no! Because Dora was coming home this Christmas with money in her bag. Money to spend! Forty dollars! Pinched off the edges of that princely allowance and swelled with those occasional hired accompaniments. Forty dollars, which she was going to spend recklessly on the aggrandizement of the Skipping home. It was a sum so large one way and so small the other that she hadn't any idea just what she would buy with it.

And let me sit beside you, in your eyes
Seeing the vision—★

A small clock on the desk said ten-thirty. Abruptly Dora disconnected the iron, uptilted it, and ran to the upper hall. She hung over the stair rail.

"Yoo-hoo!" she called softly but penetratingly to a dark head two stories below and smiled seraphically at a familiar upturned face. "Marge, would you mind seeing if there's mail for me?"

"I'm on my way with it," said the one called Marge, her voice rich with the sarcasm of a knowing contemporary. "Your daily special!"

The letter which Dora presently carried back to her steamy laundry to read was brief. "Sweetheart," it said,

★"Oh, Promise Me" comes from the 1889 comic operetta *Robin Hood*. Reginald De Koven wrote the music; Clement Scott wrote the lyrics.

"I love you. See you tonight. I can manage three days off next week. Yours forever, Fred."

※ ※ ※

It was on the train homeward bound that Dora experienced her first twinge of uncertainty about Fred and his visit. She was riding in the day coach for economy. Fred had put her on the train. He had wanted to buy her a Pullman reservation, but she wouldn't allow it.

"Some day," she coaxed, "I shall love for you to, but not now—you understand?"

And Fred had been nice—he was always nice—but troubled.

That worried Dora, a little. Exuberance, she thought, was a dangerous feeling. It blinded one to realities. Realities were being looked at awfully hard nowadays. Fred's shining eyes had strayed once or twice from her to her surroundings this morning. And the day coach was quite clean and not nearly so messed with terrible people as she had known it to be on occasions, as it likely would be later on this day. Fred's mouth had tightened.

Wait a year? his expression said. *I guess not! I'll take you out of this or know why.*

Of course she had been perfectly honest all the time that Fred was falling in love with her. Yes, honest; but extremely at her best. Because she knew right well that she had fallen in love first. He was such a nice, straight, handsome he-person! The leading incentive for fussing with frills and slicking her wardrobe had been that glimmer in Fred's eyes when he beheld her. Of course, without this incentive she would still have been Dora Skipping and charming, but not quite—so charming!

"We are fine people!" she said stoutly, half-impatient with herself this day.

❊ ❊ ❊

Still she was worried. He—Fred—would be getting a swift, sudden first impression. She had grown up with the peculiar shabby fineness of the Skippings. And her worry now was not that anything about her home or family would jar Fred's love for her. If he had been that kind of man, his opinion about anything would never have mattered to Dora. And it would have been low for her to be anxious about her family's pleasing her fiancé. Her worry was lest this precious family should receive any little hurt in this first visit. For the sake of these splendid people who had been her entire background and foreground until she had met Fred, she didn't want one flicker of such a look as that young man had given the day coach.

Fred was human. He had always lived in abundance. When she had tried to explain to him about her circumstances, she couldn't be sure he was hearing her words exactly.

"Why," she had said, "in our home we used to have to keep careful record so that we'd know whose turn it was to get the next pair of shoes."

And he had nodded and gone on looking dreamily at her hair. Oh, he was a dear! She loved him utterly; but being Dora, she championed fiercely, too, the people who had made, she thought, her life what it was; had made her for Fred; who were welcoming him, not as a disappointment to any high hopes, but as a sort of reward. If her two loyalties came into conflict, the least conflict, what should she do?

And then Dora laughed to herself. She said she was a silly one, insisting on making misery out of joy. Besides, hadn't she that forty dollars?

Her brother Paul met her at the train. He yanked her off the top step of the coach, clear of the brakeman's wooden box.

"'Lo, Sis!" he shouted in that tremendous voice that had been his the past three years. He crushed her ribs in a hug to match. He grinned all over his dark countenance—the family could never say whether Paul was homely or handsome—kissed her abruptly, and was off like a streak, her suitcase swinging at the end of one arm. What an arm! What legs! People turned and smiled at their striding progress through the waiting room.

❋ ❋ ❋

"Dr. Skipping's children," she heard someone say, someone she hadn't time to see. "Home—holidays—that boy!"

Dora took mental note of her brother's black unhatted hair and his blue and green tucked-in sweater. She'd just have to keep those items in sight somehow—and suddenly he stopped.

"There she is!" he announced, and threw her baggage recklessly into the rear vacancy of a—well—an automobile.

Fundamentally the vehicle had been an old-type Ford. The various additions and substitutions only its final designer could have traced and named. Dora knew that it looked strange somehow, anyhow, and wondered what she might ever be able to say of the paint job. The whole thing had been painted to a brilliancy of new patent leather.

"Paul—a car?" she gasped. "Not yours?"

"Part mine," he claimed proudly. "Nick Sherer's and mine. He bought the works. I put them together. He buys the gas and oil and whatnot. I do the tinkering. We both of us have the use of it. Nick's got a new business. Plans to use this contraption for delivery part time. Thought maybe you'd help us think up a smart slogan for the rear."

The ruined top, Paul explained superfluously, had been sawed off a sedan to make the present open-car style. That offered a rear expanse for painting information about Nick Sherer's new cleaning and dyeing company.

"Well, there she is!" roared Paul. "Skip in, Miss Skipping!"

Dora, as she tried to sit lightly on the shiny cushions that did look as if they might be sticky, was remembering Fred's straight eight-cylinder.

"Oh, Paul!" she sighed. "I'd forgotten how good you are at this sort of thing."

"Yeah," he answered over the uproar of the starting motor. "Just listen to that, will you? Sweet? You bet!"

Presently he added, "That fellow of yours—didn't you say he was an electrician? Well, there's something I want to ask him about this generator."

"Paul, you're wonderful!" said Dora.

One thing was settled. It would take many times forty dollars to eliminate this particular automobile from the family.

St. Joseph was so old-fashioned that a preacher's house was still called a parsonage. The Skipping home was an old red brick mansion with a white porch all across the front that was painted by subscription every third spring. The third spring was approaching and not any too soon; but the lines of the house were good and gracious and welcoming, and it might snow over Christmas to hide broken lattices and bleak bare vines.

When Dora opened the front door, there was the warm brown smell of fresh gingerbread on the air; and a woman's voice, low and almost a warble for sweetness, was mocking somebody over the telephone: "Perfectly lovely! The darling little imps of Satan in their white angel robes marching up two by two with candles, one stanza behind the organist, because two or three will have mislaid their candles or the Widow Jones will have had a window opened because of her asthma and the draft will have blown—"

"Mother!" cried Dora.

The receiver clicked sharply, abruptly.

"My beautiful daughter! My lamb returned to the fold—"

But Mrs. Skipping trembled ever so little in Dora's embrace and her lips quivered. *She is the loveliest person in the world,* Dora had always thought. Her crisp black hair was snow-powdered now. Her face was etched with lines of large and small pains and pangs that she had always kept quite to herself. Her mouth was firm and proud and young. Her black eyes snapped and twinkled. Her figure, even in its almost continual print housedress, was as slim and straight as ever, Dora thought, not knowing how slim a girl could be a generation back.

Mrs. Skipping was really small, however, not nearly so tall as Dora.

"Was there ever a woman so completely overgrown with children?" she sighed, contemplating her oldest daughter. "Paul! Paul, what are you doing with your sister's fitted dressing case? Do you want to break every cut-glass bottle in it?"

"Is there—" Paul lifted the cowhide bag and surveyed it with wonder before he comprehended his mother's irony. "Aw!" he rebuked her.

❄ ❄ ❄

"Home!" said Dora with a relish, as if she tasted something even better than hot gingerbread; and then there was a scraping on the upstairs' floor that sent her flying with the quick instinct sharpened by years of familiarity up to greet her sister Gretel, who had been crippled from infancy but who would go up and down stairs as often as anyone asked her to or wanted her where she wasn't—dark, beautiful Gretel, with the cropped hair and haunting eyes of a boy poet.

After Gretel there was Felix. Felix was another girl, the twelve-year-old baby of the house. It just happened that when Felix was expected the half-dozen brothers and sisters waited for her as hopefully as the parents, and they had chosen the name for the coming baby. Later it was feared that a change in name might bring bad luck; so Felix the little girl was called. She was a weedy child now, with Dora's coloring, but fearful promise of a build similar to Paul's. Her line was drawing. When Dora had left home in the fall she was doing sunsets.

Now the specialty was silhouettes. John Barrymore and
the Washingtons fairly papered the walls of the room
she shared with sweet-tempered Gretel.

This was Dora's family, all except her father. There
was still the house. It was clean and comfortable and
warm, but very bare. There was no luxury of silken drap-
eries or deep-cushioned couches. Chairs and tables had
been bought for service or had been presented by congre-
gations with the idea that they must last a long time.
They were stout plain chairs and tables, their varying
styles writing a history of furniture-making in the last
three decades, their scars like runes telling a tale of growing, lively children. The old black grand piano, filling
one-third of the living room, loomed ponderous and
incongruously rich against the general spruce shabbiness.
Rugs were spread over the downstairs' floors now; but
the upstairs' rooms boasted only islands of woven rags.
The carpets below, for that matter, had been worn to the
backing in spots where feet rested most continually. They
had been turned and turned around until now there was
no choice between thin spots. The kitchen linoleum
needed replacement. Everything was like that. No
church, whatever its pride, unless it was a church too
proud to appreciate a Dr. Skipping, could hope to supply
the needs of a family that would squander its substance on
musical educations and the like.

❄ ❄ ❄

Dinner was ready before Dr. Skipping returned. Dora
helped to set the table. "Please!" she begged; and then
she went about putting out silver and china and glass,

very, very thoughtfully. The meal would be simple, but fastidious and exquisitely served. Silver, if counted carefully against loss, doesn't wear out. Linen, if laundered kindly, remains fine linen to the last thread. There were candles in silver candlesticks and a rose in a bud vase. It was a Skipping idea that the flavor of food depended largely on environment. But the food would be good, too. Nobody could adorn a bargain roast with better, richer gravy than could Mrs. Skipping; and tonight there would be the hot gingerbread, made from real cane syrup shipped from the South for Christmas. Dinner at the Skippings was their triumphant declaration that the fineness of living had survived all tests.

With every touch that she gave the table Dora fell more and more quiet. A cold realization came to weigh on her heart until she wondered if she would be able to eat later. She knew now why she had waited so long to admit to Fred and to herself that she loved him. She couldn't marry—anyone—not for ever so long. A year, why, a year would be nothing. If she worked ten years and was enormously successful, she couldn't give those dear ones all the treasures she ached to shower upon them. They were people deserving better than privation, and privation had been the keynote of their existence. She must make up the deficit, she, to whom they had all given without reproaching her so much as with a consciousness that they were giving, must give in return, largely.

Just as her mood was verging on the somber, Dora jerked herself up. It would not do to be sorrowful on her homecoming. This horrible decision about Fred was a thing to be put away until she was fast in her own small bedroom for the night. Now, now she must think of something else and quickly. What? The forty dollars, of course! The forty dollars with which she had planned to glorify the house. Now it would be just the first of many gifts. Dora blinked and cast her eyes about.

The possibilities were overwhelming. There was, first, the everlasting problem of carpets. She might find downtown a few small rugs in soft, bright colors for the most prominent worn places. They wouldn't be Oriental rugs but would be good velvet carpetings. She might find two of them, say, and with the rest of the money buy Gretel a frame and the yarns and a pattern for a hooked rug. That would be a present to Gretel, too, the lovely work for her hands. Or might she find a real bargain in a good cushioned chair? Probably not. Furniture was so expensive! Later for that. Or a lamp of hand-wrought iron, perhaps; and a soft-hued shade for one beautiful corner at night? No. The family would stand the lamp at the piano and place her under its radiance and—that wasn't the idea! Curtains? She could buy yards and yards of silk, and Gretel, again, would be happy to do the sewing. Perhaps the curtains would be best. She'd have to make a list of possibilities and see how far the forty dollars would go.

This bit of woman's planning brightened Dora's eyes and lifted her mouth corners until she looked quite happy as she went back to the living room where Mrs. Skipping was awaiting the hour for serving dinner and trying to help Paul decide between two offers of positions—one as assistant operator in the latest moving picture theater, the other as working partner in Nick Sherer's new cleaning business.

"And remember," she mocked affectionately, "don't

let friendship lure you from the shining ways of art, dear. Now money—that would be different!"

"Aw!" said Paul adoring her, but helpless under her teasing.

"What is keeping Dad?" asked Dora.

"Heaven knows," said Mrs. Skipping. "I mean that literally, darling. When the Reverend Dr. Skipping leaves home in the morning, I say a special prayer to our heavenly Father to bring him back to us safely. The Reverend, left to himself, would never accomplish it. He'd get so lost among his blessed works—"

A breath of cold air swept in from the hall.

"Is that so?" challenged a rich, deep voice borne in on the draft.

Dora waited, not to miss the glimmer that came to her mother's eyes at any sudden appearance of the father, the warming, the softening that came all over her face.

❄ ❄ ❄

Dr. Skipping had taken off his overcoat. He was unwinding a muffler and beaming in the general direction of family chatter. Somehow the picture of him standing there smote home to Dora's heart. Another indelible impression, like that picture of John before he went to war. He looked at once so young and so old, this father of hers. He'd always seemed just young before, young and strong and ruddy with health, if never exactly handsome; but now—she wondered just what his years might be. His hair was thinning rapidly. The glinting gold of her own head was bleached sand on her father's. The lenses of his glasses—had he needed them strengthened again this winter? So soon. His broad shoulders were always a little stooped—they looked bowed today. Perhaps it was just the way he had put on his coat.

That dear man and his clothes! It was a blessing he had an orator's voice and a pleasing personality or no church of any dignity would ever have claimed him as he walked about the streets, he was so baggy in the knees.

Not that Dora or anybody really minded about his clothes. Not that he minded. Serenely oblivious to bagged knees and uneven coattails, Dr. Skipping held out his arms in welcome.

"My dad!" Dora said with a strangled gulp, strangled, because Skippings never carried on.

"Well, well!" Her father shook her gently and held her off after kissing her. "And have you been in the house two hours and no kind person told you about the smudge on your face?" He pulled out a handkerchief and painstakingly wiped off the one tear that she hadn't been able to hold back.

❋ ❋ ❋

The next day Dora had lunch downtown with her father. In the late afternoon, when the family was sniffing about the kitchen and making eyes at two cherry pies—Mrs. Skipping said at mealtimes they were like orphans with their noses against the windowpanes—Dora heard a tapping on the front door glass and let her father into the main hall unobserved. Fifteen minutes later Mrs. Skipping sat down for the usual before-dinner lull.

"We will not wait for your blessed father," she announced.

"Dad is at home," said Dora. "No, wait a minute. I want to tell you something."

She tried not to strike a pose, but this was a momentous occasion.

"At school this past term," she said, "I managed to save forty dollars from my allowance. I brought it home and I spent it all today on a present for the house."

There was silence.

"Daughter," said Mrs. Skipping weakly or in pretense of weakness, "*forty dollars*—all in one day?"

"No kidding!" said Paul. "What did you get?"

"Dora, Dora!" said Mrs. Skipping. "Why didn't you tell me? There's been a dancing frock at Beutel's that I've wanted for you since the Thanksgiving sales."

"Now, Mother!"

"Oh, but I wouldn't have let you buy things for the house! I want you to have your pretties, now. Why, I remember the first time your father took me to a theater, I spent all my month's allowance on one hat. The play was a sad one and I cried on the ribbons, but I never regretted the extravagance. I still have the hat. Dora, I would have made you get that dress and perhaps some new slippers."

"Mother's sparring for time," said Paul. "What did you get?"

"Father has it upstairs," said Dora, hugging her mother close.

"Well, he'll never remember to bring it down if you don't remind him," said Mrs. Skipping. "Paul, elevate your basso profundo and call the dear man."

Obediently Paul rose, one hand tugging at the belt of his trousers.

"I said elevate your basso profundo, Paul."

"Well, I am!" With both hands Paul jerked at the belt.

"Your basso profundo, dear, is your deep bass voice."

"Aw!" said Paul, amid general excited laughing. "If you would ever call pants *pants*, a fellow wouldn't get so mixed!"

He went up the steps three at a time. There was a shout about the moment when he should have hit the upper hall, and down he clattered backward with imminent danger to his own neck and everything else breakable in the general vicinity.

"My cat's eyebrows!" he gasped. "Do you see what I see?"

Down the steps after him advanced with dignity and yet with a certain snap, a most distinguished gentleman in a brand new custom-tailored suit. It had to be a black suit, but it was the smartest and latest cut. Dr. Skipping looked like a model from the front page of an advertising section—and he knew it. Had anybody thought him oblivious to his shabbiness? That person needed to see him now. He could have preened no more in the day of his first long pants. The stoop seemed to have lifted from his shoulders. He beamed and invited his gasping family to view him on all sides, to feel that cloth! Hadn't he and Dora found a tremendous bargain? Didn't he look grand?

Mrs. Skipping cried.

"Paul," she said, while the tears still ran, "immediately after supper you're to fetch those abominable rags he has shed and burn them. Will you, dear?"

But Felix precipitated the denouement.

"I know!" she squealed. "Dora wanted to dress up the house for her sweetheart, but she changed her mind and dressed up Father."

Dora swallowed hard. The family had to be told—something.

"I'm not sure that Fred is coming," she faltered.

"What?" The cry seemed to assail her from all sides at once. It carried every shade of disappointment, unbelief, protest. Mrs. Skipping stiffened. There was no light mockery in her then. But perhaps the sharpest exclamation was from Gretel, who, last night, had made Dora's battle very hard by creeping into her room and asking to be told all about the wonderful man. Poor Gretel!

❋ ❋ ❋

"I telegraphed him last night." Dora wondered how she could explain.

"Pooh!" said Dr. Skipping. "Of course he's coming. What's a letter? I've been talking to him over the telephone."

"But you don't know what I said in my letter—"

"Yes, I do. He told me. I'd have known anyhow. We talked and between us we decided not to pay any attention to the letter, or to any other sacrificial arguments you might put up. We decided that we were the men of the family. Why, the only reason I bought this suit was so that I might look respectable at your wedding!"

The glimmer was strong on Mrs. Skipping's face. She laid hold of her husband's arm. Dora laid hold of the other.

"Daddy Skipping," she said, "there were three dollars

left of the suit money. Did you or did you not get that new shirt as you promised?"

"I did not," said the Reverend. "I've got lots of shirts, but only one prospective son-in-law. And he's due here at eight-thirty this evening. Not tomorrow or the day after, but tonight. Our conversation was worth more than three dollars. So, let's have dinner and let me get off to meet that train. Did you think I dressed up like this just to show off before you all?"

Shirley Seifert
(1889–1971)

Shirley Seifert, prominent novelist and short story writer, was born in St. Peters, Missouri. Among her best-selling novels are *Land of Tomorrow* (1937), *River Out of Eden* (1940), and *Look to the Rose* (1960).

Michael L. Lindvall

THE CHRISTMAS PAGEANT

For forty-six years, the church Christmas pageant ran like clockwork. Everything tied to a script that left no room for error—each was a near-perfect production.

But finally came a Christmas where the unexpected occurred. The results could have been foreseen.

Well, some of them. . . .

❄ ❄ ❄

*T*he Christmas pageant is over. It was, in the end, wonderful, and now that it is past, my blood pressure and, in fact, the church's communal blood pressure have dropped about twenty points. We got through it again without schism and with no divorces. None of the kids got grounded this year, but it was close.

The whole saga of the Christmas pageant really began precisely forty-seven Christmases ago when Alvina Johnson first directed Second Presbyterian's children's Christmas pageant, something that she continued to do through ten pastors, nine U.S. presidents, three wars, and who knows how many Christian education committees, for the next forty-six years— but not this year, and that's the story. International alliances came and went; wars were fought and peace made; ministers were called and then called away—but Alvina Johnson directing the children's Christmas pageant was like a great rock in a turbulent sea.

Alvina is "Mrs. Johnson," although there is no "Mr. Johnson." There was a Mr. Johnson for only three and a half weeks, forty-nine years ago. A few days shy of their month's wedding anniversary, Mr. Johnson (nobody remembers his first name) left, although Alvina never puts it that way. She prefers to say, "He just ran off to Minneapolis."

One might call Alvina "stubborn," but that word isn't quite enough. Alvina is intractable, intransigent, unmovable. When folks around here get put out with Alvina, who is disguised as a sweet and demure seventy-year-old lady, they refer to her, under their breath of course, as "the iron butterfly."

But Alvina does what she says, always, exactly, and

forever. Forty-seven years ago somebody asked her to do the Christmas pageant. She said yes. They didn't say, "Would you do the Christmas pageant this year?" so Alvina, who is a literalist in all things, assumed that they meant forever, and she is a woman of her word.

Alvina's pageants always had precisely nine characters: one Mary, one Joseph, three wise men, two shepherds, one angel, and one narrator.

The script was simply the Christmas story out of the King James Bible, which meant that two six-year-old shepherds had to learn to say, "Let us now go even unto Bethlehem, and see this thing which is come to pass, which the Lord hath made known unto us."

Auditions for the nine parts were held the last Sunday afternoon in October for forty-six years. Rehearsals for the nine lucky winners were held for the next five Sunday afternoons. Alvina's goal was nothing less than perfection in Christmas pageantry: perfect lines, perfect pacing, perfect blocking, perfect enunciation, perfect everything, which is not easily achieved with little children, even nine carefully selected ones. Critics said that Alvina would have much preferred working with nine midget actors, if she could have gotten away with it.

Time and again people tried to get Alvina to open things up so that every kid who wanted a part could have one. "Alvina," they would say, "Scripture says that there was a heavenly host, not just one lonely angel. Alvina, why not a few more shepherds, then everybody could be in the pageant?" or "Alvina, if there were shepherds, there had to be sheep, right? We'll make some cute little woolly sheep outfits for the three- and four-year-olds." "Nope," she'd answer, "too many youngsters, too many problems."

Early in the fall, however, something happened that deflected the inertia of nearly half a century of always doing it the way it had always been done. The Christian education committee included the three young mothers of last year's rejected Mary, Joseph, and Wise Man Number Two. And these young mothers pulled off what they call in Central America a coup d'état. At their September meeting they passed the following motion: "Resolved: All children who wish to be in the Christmas pageant may do so. Parts will be found."

Alvina heard about it that night and was in my office the next morning at nine o'clock sharp. She began by asking me if I thought the decorations on the Christmas tree in the church parlor were appropriate. I had not noticed them, I said. Well, she informed me, they were walnut shells decorated to look like little mice with tiny stocking caps on their heads. "What," she asked, "do mice have to do with the birth of our Lord?"

Now, I knew this wasn't the problem. I, too, had heard about the committee meeting the night before. "What's the matter, Alvina?" I asked. "Young mothers," she said. She spit these two words out as though "young mother" were an illicit occupation. "Young mothers," she continued, "who have no knowledge or experience in the proper direction of a Christmas pageant. Young mothers are behind those walnut-shell mice, and they are behind the destruction of the Christmas pageant." She then resigned as director and said, "If these young mothers know so much, let them try to do it." She was angry, maybe even angry enough to quit

the church and become a Methodist, but she didn't.
I suspect that she wanted to hang around at least long
enough to see the young mothers fall flat on their faces.

The pageant was last week. The young mothers
didn't fall flat on their faces, but the pageant was, well,
different from what everybody had come to expect over
the last forty-six years. It seemed as though there were a
cast of thousands, even though the actual number was
fifty or so, which was every kid in the church up to
about eighth grade. At this age, they would sooner die
than get dressed up in the father's bathrobe and pretend
to be a biblical character.

There must have been a dozen shepherds and ten
angels (a veritable heavenly host). Then there were the
sheep, a couple dozen three-, four-, and five-year-olds
who had on woolly, fake-sheepskin vests with woolly
hoods and their dads' black socks pulled up on their
arms and legs. The pageant was a lot of things, but
smooth it wasn't. And one of the chief problems was
these very sheep. Now, in suburban Christmas pageants,
I imagine sheep are well behaved and fairly quiet, but
suburban kids have seldom seen real sheep. The only
sheep most suburban kids have ever seen are on the
front of Sunday church bulletin covers: peaceful, grazing
sheep who just stand there and look cute and cuddly.

Half of the kids here live on farms. They've seen real
sheep, many of them. They know that sheep don't just
stand there. They know that sheep don't often follow
directions. They know that sheep are dumb. They
know that all sheep want to do is eat.

So, when the young mothers casually instructed the
two dozen sheep to act like sheep, they really should

have known better. Some of the sheep started to do a remarkable imitation of grazing behind the communion table. Some wandered over by the choir to graze, and others went down the center aisle. Some of them had donuts they found in the church parlor to make their grazing look even more realistic. When one of the shepherds tried to herd them a bit with his shepherd's crook, some of the sheep spooked and started to scatter just as real sheep do. Everybody knows that's how sheep act. It was, in fact, a remarkable imitation of sheep behavior, even though a bit out of the ordinary for a Christmas pageant.

Now, Alvina was watching all this from the last pew of the sanctuary. I could just see her from where I was sitting. As the sheep spooked and scattered with much imitation bleating, Alvina looked down to hide a smirk. *Young mothers*, I'm sure she was thinking. *If they know so much, let them try to direct the Christmas pageant.* The real climax of imprecision came, however, at that point of high drama when Mary and Joseph enter, Mary clutching a baby doll in a blue blanket. This year's Mary, whose name was actually Mary, was taking her role with an intense and pious seriousness. She looked into the face of the doll in her arms with eyes that really seemed to see the infant Christ. Joseph was another story. He had gotten the part because he had been rejected from Christmas pageant participation by Alvina Johnson more times than any other kid in church "With good reason," some might say.

Anyway, Mary and Joseph were to walk on as the narrator read, "And Joseph also went up from Galilee, out of the city of Nazareth, into Judea, unto the city of

David, which is called Bethlehem . . . to be taxed with Mary his espoused wife, being great with child." At least this is what the narrator was *supposed* to read. It was what the narrator had read at the rehearsal. But a few hours before the performance, one of the young mothers had observed that none of the children could much understand King James English, so they voted, in their ongoing mood of revolutionary fervor, to switch to the Good News translation of the Bible for the performance. "What kid knows what 'great with child' means?" they asked.

The newly chosen translation is much more direct at this point. So, as Mary and Joseph entered, the narrator read, "Joseph went to register with Mary who was promised in marriage to him. She was pregnant."

As that last word echoed from the narrator through the PA system into the full church, our little Joseph, hearing it, frozen in his tracks, gave Mary an incredulous look, peered out at the congregation, and said, "Pregnant? What do you mean, pregnant?" This, of course, brought down the house. My wife, wiping tears from her eyes, leaned over to me and said, "You know, that may well be just what Joseph actually said."

Alvina was now wearing a look that simply broadcast, *I told you so*. But as the pageant wound into its closing tableaux and the church lights were dimmed for the singing of "Silent Night," a couple of magical—I would allow, miraculous—things happened. The sheep, when they had finished with their part, bleated their way down the aisle to sit in the last couple of pews to watch the end of the pageant. Alvina was in the last pew, and she suddenly found herself surrounded by a little herd of three-, four-, and five-year-olds in sheep outfits.

It was late, the church was warm, and the sheep were drowsy. I glanced over at Alvina as the wise men were exiting and the organ was softly playing the melody of "Silent Night." The sheep in the pew on either side of Alvina had fallen asleep and were resting their fake-wool heads on her shoulders, something they would feel comfortable doing with any grown-up in church. As the church went dark for the singing of "Silent Night," we could see what had been happening outside for the last hour. The first real snow of the winter was falling. Big, fat flakes floated down and covered everything with a white, uniform perfection. As we—little kids and grown-ups— saw it, there was a spontaneous and corporate "ahh."

We sang: "Silent night, holy night, All is calm, all is bright." It was very softly that we sang and all the sheep were quiet, even the ones who were awake, and everybody looked at the snow. It was as if flakes of grace were falling, falling free out of heaven and blessing the muddy earth with purity, a whiteness covering the dirt and the shoddiness with perfection. When the carol was finished, no one stirred for a long time. It wasn't planned, but we all just sat there and watched.

It seemed like an eternity, but it was maybe two minutes. Minnie MacDowell broke the spell. She's hard of hearing and always talks too loud. She meant to whisper to her husband, but everybody heard. "Perfect," she said, "just perfect."

And so it was—not perfect in the way Alvina's pageants tried to make things perfect, but perfect in the way God makes things perfect. God accepts our fumbling attempts at performance, at love and fairness, and then covers them with grace. I think the moment may have even touched the iron butterfly. Minnie said that Alvina mentioned to her that if they needed any more sheep outfits for next year, she could perhaps find time to make a few.

Michael L. Lindvall

Michael L. Lindvall, graduate of Princeton Seminary, is today senior pastor of Brick Presbyterian Church in New York City.

Arthur Maxwell

THE HOUSE THAT GLOWED

It was bitterly cold that Christmas Eve, and the freezing little boy had been turned away at house after house. Finally, he decided that there was no alternative but to die in the snow.

Yet there was one house left—a tiny, tumbledown cottage. Hoping against hope, he decided to try one last time.

✳ ✳ ✳

*I*t was Christmas Eve, and poor little Johann, driven out of his home by an angry and brutal stepfather, was trudging wearily through the snow.

His ragged coat was sodden with melted snow. His shoes were split at the seams, so that his feet were damp and numb with cold. His quaint cap, pulled down well over his ears and forehead, had a gaping tear that let in the biting wind.

Night was falling, and the gathering darkness found the homeless little boy still plodding on his sad and lonely way.

If only I could find some shelter, some place where I could get warm and the wind would not chill me so, he thought to himself. *If only someone would give me some food to eat and something hot to drink!*

Coming to the edge of the forest, he caught sight of a little village nestling in the valley below, with several fine, large houses dotting the hills around it. Lights were already twinkling in the windows, while the smoke from many chimneys, curling upward, blended with the murky sky.

A great new hope sprang up in little Johann's heart. Here at last, among so many lovely homes, he would surely find someone to care for him. He walked more quickly, certain that his troubles were almost over.

Soon he came to the entrance of a fine, big mansion. There were many lights in the windows and a very bright one over the front door. *Surely,* he thought, *people who could live in such a house must have lots of money and would be only too pleased to help a poor, hungry little boy.*

Very bravely he walked up to the front door and, by standing on tiptoe, managed to reach the bell. He pushed it hard, and there was such a noise inside that it frightened him. But he was more frightened still when the great oak door was thrown back and a big man dressed in a fine blue and gold uniform looked out at him.

"Did you ring that bell?" asked the haughty butler, frowning.

"Y-y-y-yes," stammered Johann. "I-I-I'm very cold and hungry, and I thought you—"

"This is Christmas Eve," snapped the butler, "and the house is full of guests. I'm sorry, but we haven't time to bother with the likes of you just now. Good night."

And the door was shut.

Oh! said Johann to himself, *I never thought anyone would do that. But perhaps they are too busy here. I must try somewhere else.*

So he walked on down into the village itself, passing by the other big mansions for fear the people inside might also be too busy to care about a hungry little boy on Christmas Eve.

From the first house he reached there came sounds of music and laughter. *These people will be friendly,* he said to himself as he knocked gently on the door. But there was so much noise inside that he had to knock again and again, each time louder than before.

At last the door swung open, and a young man wearing a funny paper cap looked out.

"Excuse me," said Johann, "but I wondered if you could—"

"Sorry," cried the jovial young man, "we're having a great Christmas Eve party in here, and we can't stop now."

"But please, please!" pleaded Johann.

"Sorry. Good night!" cried the young man. And *bang!* The door was shut.

Terribly disappointed, Johann went next door, but the people there were making so much noise that they didn't even hear him at all, loud as he knocked.

At the next house a crabby old gentleman looked out an upstairs window and told him to run home and not bother the neighbors. Run home, indeed!

At another house he was told to call again another day. They would help him then perhaps, the people said. But he needed help *now*!

So, going from house to house through the entire village, he sought shelter and food, and found none.

Almost hopeless and heartbroken, he trudged on into the night, leaving the twinkling lights behind him. He felt he could lie down and die in the road, he was so tired, so hungry, so discouraged.

Just then he happened to look up and found himself passing a tiny, tumbledown old cottage, so dark and dismal that he probably wouldn't have seen it at all but for the white carpet of snow on the ground showing it up. A blind almost covered the one window, letting only a faint streak of light show through at the bottom.

Johann stood still and wondered what he should do. Should he knock here?

What would be the use? Surely if the people who lived in all the big houses—who had money for lovely parties and things—couldn't afford to help a poor boy, how could the folks in a house like this? No, it was of no use. Better not bother them. Better go on and die in the woods.

Then he thought again. He had knocked at so many houses, there could be no harm in trying one more. So he turned from the road up the snow-covered garden path and tapped gently on the door.

A moment later the door opened cautiously, and an elderly woman peered out. "Bless my soul!" she exclaimed. "Whatever are you doing out there in the cold tonight?"

"Please—" began Johann.

But before he could say another word, she had flung the door wide open and dragged him inside.

"You poor little child!" she exclaimed. "Deary, deary me! You look so cold and hungry. Half-starved, or I'm mistaken. And wet clear through. Let's get those things off at once. Wait a moment while I stir up the fire and put the kettle on."

Johann looked about him and saw that the little one-roomed cottage was as bare as could be, without even a carpet on the floor. The light he had seen came from one lone candle set on the mantelpiece. But he hadn't time to see much else, for the kind woman was soon stripping off his wet rags, wrapping him in a blanket, and setting him up at the table before a bowl of steaming soup.

Then she went back to stir the pot on the stove. As she did so she suddenly noticed that something strange was happening. She looked up.

Was it a dream, or were her eyes deceiving her? The candlelight had given place to a warm and lovely glow that seemed to be getting brighter every minute, filling every corner of the cottage with a heavenly radiance. Every drab piece of furniture seemed to be shining and glistening like burnished gold, as when God filled the Temple with His glory.

And the rich man, looking down from his mansion on

the hill, suddenly exclaimed. "There's a strange light in the valley. Look! Widow Greatheart's cottage is on fire!"

The news spread swiftly from house to house, and soon all the merry parties were abandoned as the people, wrapping themselves up in their coats and shawls, rushed out to see what was the matter.

They saw the light, too, and running toward the widow's cottage, beheld the poor tumbledown old building glowing like an alabaster bowl. Very excited, they gathered around it.

Peering inside, all they could see was the dear old woman caring for the very same little boy who had called that night at so many of their homes.

Then, as the light faded, they knocked on the door to ask anxiously what could have happened.

"I really don't know," said Widow Greatheart, with a smile of wondrous joy and satisfaction on her face. "I just seemed to hear a voice saying to me, 'Inasmuch as you have done it unto one of the least of these My children, you have done it unto Me.'"

Arthur S. Maxwell
(1896–1970)

Arthur S. Maxwell spent the first forty years of his life in England and the last thirty-four in America. One of the most prolific writers of his time, he wrote 112 books that have been printed in fifty-six languages and fifty-one countries. A staggering total of 85 million copies of his books have been sold. His all-time best sellers are the *Uncle Arthur Bedtime Stories* (45 million) and *The Bible Story* series (30 million).

As Retold by Albert P. Stauderman

PLEASE, SIR, I WANT
TO BUY A MIRACLE

What is the price of a miracle?

Exactly $1.11.

✳ ✳ ✳

Throughout the big city there was gaiety and laughter, for it was the morning of a Christmas Day. But no tree, no tinsel, and no gifts marked the holiday in a crowded tenement flat where a little boy lay deathly ill on a cot.

His parents watched in speechless anguish as the young doctor carefully examined the small patient. A serious spinal infection was drawing the last strength from the young body. Finally the doctor stood up and turned to place his stethoscope in his bag. From the sorrow of his own heart, without looking at the parents, he spoke softly and slowly, "Only a miracle can save him now."

In the doorway, wide-eyed and frightened, stood a little girl. In her childish way she shared the grief of her parents when she heard the doctor's words. "Only a miracle," he had said. That must mean another of those expensive treatments that they could never afford.

She gulped back tears and ran to her own room. There, on the table, was the dollar she had been given for Christmas. From her bank she shook out eleven pennies, its entire contents. It seemed like a small fortune: $1.11, and all hers to spend as she liked!

Carefully she clutched the money and ran down the stairs and out the back door, out into the wintry street. A few wandering snowflakes brushed softly against her face as she darted down the block. Breathlessly she pushed her way into the corner drugstore.

At the counter in the rear of the store the friendly, old white-haired druggist was talking to a big man in a huge fur coat. She stood there impatiently for a few minutes while the men continued to talk. Then she rapped on the counter with her pennies. She knew it wasn't polite to interrupt, but her need was urgent.

"Please, sir," she implored, *"I want to buy a miracle."* The conversation ceased abruptly as both men looked down at her. The druggist knew her family well. For weeks they had been buying all sorts of medicines for their sick child.

"What did you say, dear?" he asked.

"The doctor says we need a miracle to save my little brother. He's very sick, so we need it right away. Look, I can pay for it."

She plunked her money down on the counter and blinked back a tear. The kindly druggist stared at her for a moment and then at the money lying on the counter. Then he turned back to the man in the fur coat and began to talk earnestly to him in big words that the little girl could hardly understand—something about spines and specialists.

The man in the fur coat cleared his throat loudly. Then he bent down and placed his hand on her shoulder.

"My dear," he said, "miracles are very hard to get, but I think I may be able to get one for you."

"Here's the money," cried the little girl eagerly, pushing her small hoard across the counter toward him.

"Mmmm . . . yes," said the big man thoughtfully, looking at the dollar bill and the pennies. "That's just the right amount. They cost exactly $1.11. Now tell me, little girl, what the name of your brother's doctor is."

Happily the little girl skipped homeward with her wonderful secret.

A few hours later the young doctor's telephone rang. It was a call from a famous specialist whom he would never have dared even approach. Through a mutual friend, the specialist said, he had been asked to inquire about the case of a sick boy.

It was still Christmas Day when they stood once more at the sick boy's little cot. The gray wintry evening darkened the single window, making the room look more drab than ever.

The troubled parents watched in bewilderment, but with a new ray of hope lighting their hearts. When the two doctors finally left, the sick boy was sleeping, and the parents knew that he would soon be in a fine hospital, with the best of care and attention and with every hope of full recovery. They couldn't understand. It seemed like a miracle.

In the doorway of the room stood the little girl, wide-eyed but no longer frightened. She understood completely what had happened. She knew something her parents didn't know. She knew that the price of a miracle was exactly one dollar and eleven cents.

Plus the faith of a little child.

Albert P. Stauderman

Albert P. Stauderman wrote during the first half of the twentieth century.

Temple Bailey

O LITTLE FLOCK

Her husband, who had always been her mainstay, was dead; her money was almost gone; and her two oldest children insisted that she spend it all for Christmas. So what would she do when all the bills came in?

Then Dr. Wade—who had loved her "for a thousand years"—stepped in.

❄ ❄ ❄

*T*he choir was practicing Christmas carols in the church next door. There are some advantages in living next to a church, even if you are in a shabby old apartment house that backs up to the sacred edifice, with a frontage on an unfashionable thoroughfare.

One advantage, Sara had found, was on moonlit nights, when you could look out upon the high, delicate spire etched against the golden sky and be flooded with a sense of the world's beauty. And another was when, in moments of deep depression, the sound of the organ swept over you in waves of celestial harmony.

At times, however, Sara felt there were no advantages. As tonight when the reiteration of the Christmas carols got on her nerves.

It is all very well, was her mental challenge, *to sing like that. As if Christmas Day made up for everything. But it doesn't. Not when you have four children. Not when every one of them wants something you can't give. Not when you haven't any money. Not when you don't dare face your bills. Not when—*

She stopped there. Why go on, with that crash of exultation weakening her protests?

> *Oh, take the gift,*
> *In joy receive;*
> *All things are His*
> *Who will believe;*
> *O little flock,*
> *What words can tell,*
> *The bliss of souls—*

It was really a beautiful carol, but Sara had no patience with it. *If they knew anything about sheep, they wouldn't talk of flocks.*

Sara knew a great deal about sheep. Her girlhood had been spent on her grandfather's old place in Virginia. His sheep had roamed the hills of Albemarle, and the animals were picturesque at long distance, but not so meek as the poets have them. Sara had once owned a pet lamb, which had shown revolutionary traits. When she wanted it to follow, it had had a way of kicking up its heels and ramping sideways down the road, leaving her dismayed and disconcerted.

And now her own little flock had kicked up its heels. And she didn't know what to do about it. She didn't know what to do about anything. If only the children knew how helpless she felt without their father.

But of course they couldn't know. They were young, and youth is thoughtless. She must seem to her children quite mature and self-sufficient. They couldn't know the panic in her heart when she thought of the years ahead of her.

She had made her Christmas plans with certainty that they would cooperate. She had felt sure that the older ones, at least, would share her sense of responsibility when the situation was explained to them.

So that very night at dinner she had said, "My darlings, some of Daddy's investments have gone wrong. I'm afraid we shall have to have a rather shabby Christmas."

"What do you mean by 'shabby'?" young Randolf, in his father's place at the head of the table, had flung out.

"Oh, well, I wondered if we couldn't go down to

Solomon's Shore for the holidays. We'd be very cozy and happy and—"

They stopped her with a chorus: "Solomon's Shore!"

No mistaking that tone of horrified protest. She tried to ignore it: "We could have the time of our lives, couldn't we?"

"We could *not*," this from Kathleen, seventeen and a beauty, "and anyhow there's my Christmas Eve party."

"My dear, I'm afraid you'll have to give that up."

"Do you mean," there was a sort of breathlessness about Kathleen, "that I am not to entertain my friends, after I've been asked *everywhere*—asked and asked and asked, and *never* paid back?"

Sara, white and troubled, demanded, "What can I do?"

Then young Randolf, cocksurely, "Kits is right, Mother. She ought to have her party, even if we have to sell the family jewels."

"But we haven't any jewels, Randy."

"Don't be so literal-minded, Mums. What I mean is, let's forget dull care at Christmastime and mortgage the house and lot."

"But we haven't any house and lot," she answered patiently.

"There you go again. It's this way. Cut out economy during the holidays, and give us a whale of a time, and we'll live on bread and cheese if we have to. Kits and I have social obligations, and they've got to be met. We want a party and clothes for it."

"Randy, I can't pay my January bills."

"Pay your February ones, then. Lots of people let them run over, and we'll take lean pickings for a month or two."

She tried to tell them it was impossible. But they bore down with their arguments until she had no strength left to combat them. Yet it was not their arguments that finally weakened her, but Kathleen's lovely face rainwashed by tears. "We'd be *buried* at Solomon's Shore, Mother. What made you think of it?"

"Your daddy and I loved it," said Sara simply, "and so did you when you were little."

"Oh, well, of course; but things are different in these days," said young Randolph. "We have to keep up with the procession."

Arguments, arguments, arguments! At last Sara told them desperately, "I'll see what I can do. I have to think of our future."

"You think too much," her son promptly assured her. "Just gather your rosebuds, old dear, and forget tomorrow."

After that helpful remark, he got up from the table, and later went off with Kathleen and some young friends to the movies, leaving Sara high and dry, as it were, on the shores of her dilemma.

After their departure, Mary Virginia, who was eight and had some lessons to do before she went to bed, looked up from her place under the lamp and said, "I think it would be dreadful if Kits couldn't."

And Bobs, the baby, being tucked in, added a codicil to his usual prayers, "Please, God, give Kits her Christmas party."

Was it any wonder that Sara, standing now by the window, listening to that triumphant choir, flung a challenge to their glorious tidings? Christmas was not a time of peace and good will. It was a time of spending more than you could afford. It was a time of trying to keep up with other people. It was a time, not of light-heartedness, but of heaviness. Yet the children were young. And youth had a right to good times and gaiety.

※ ※ ※

Having a Liberty Bond or two, Sara sold them. She sold them in order that Kits might have her party and Randy his first dress clothes. Kathleen, flaming into more-than-ever loveliness, said, "Oh, Mother, you're a darling," and Randy patted her on the back and called her a good sport.

Well, of course it was something to be approved by your children. Sara told herself with a touch of sarcasm that mothers had stolen for less. She was amazed to find herself appreciating the satire of the situation. Having had their own way, Randy and Kathleen proceeded to show their mother they adored her for letting them have it. They led her on into further extravagances. Kits's party, they said, must be the real thing. No homemade sandwiches and salads. Old Martha, their cook, might do for every day, but not for this occasion. A caterer must do it all. "We might as well be killed for a sheep as a lamb," Randy proclaimed grandiloquently.

Being again reminded of flocks and fleece, Sara wanted to retort that you couldn't eat your mutton and have it, too. But she refrained. She knew the futility of attempting to stem the tide of Randy's disputations.

She was, however, not happy. She was oppressed by a sense of her lack of proper guardianship. What if they were wrecked on the shoals of debt? Who would save them? And wouldn't it be her fault if they went under?

She lay awake nights thinking about it. At last she showed dark circles under eyes, an unwonted paleness.

One morning, coming to the breakfast table with a blinding headache, she seemed so worn and spent that Randy asked solicitously, "Aren't you well?"

"Yes. Why?"

"You don't look it. You'd better see Wade Phillips."

But Sara didn't want to see Wade. She knew he would say at once, "It's those children. They're draining the life out of you."

Wade had been a friend and college chum of her husband, and was the family doctor. He was also Sara's adviser and friend. He didn't approve of Sara's attitude toward her children. "You're too good to them," he told her, "and they take advantage of it. They'd be a lot better off if you'd treat 'em rough."

She flamed and said, "I want them to love me."

"They'll love you more if you don't let them impose on you. You've got to show them that you're the head of the house."

He embroidered this theme somewhat one night when he came to look at Mary Virginia's tonsils. "Parents," he remarked with a spoon in Mary Virginia's mouth, "ought to be mid-Victorian."

Mary Virginia, regaining presently the use of her tongue, demanded, "What's mid-Victorian?"

"Well, those were the days when little children had to mind their mothers."

"I do mind her."

"You didn't when you wouldn't wear your overshoes

and got your feet wet. And now Mother has to nurse you. If you and Bobby and Kits and Randy were mine I'd shut you up in cages."

Mary Virginia was entranced. "*Would* you?"

"Yes. And it wouldn't be as nice as you think," he replied, adding, "And if you get your feet wet again I'll cut out your tonsils."

With that he left her and went downstairs with Sara. "What have you been doing to yourself?" he asked, as they stood in front of the fire.

"Why?"

"You look as if a puff of wind would blow you away."

"I'm a little tired, that's all."

"I'll bet those irresponsible offspring of yours are acting up."

"I wish you wouldn't call them names. If they are troublesome, it's my fault."

"Nonsense; I'd manage them."

"You *do* manage them," she said, "and the more you bully them the more they adore you."

He laughed a little, but his eyes had a softened look. "I only bully them," he said, "when I have a just cause. And they know it."

In the moment's silence which followed, the voices of the choir broke in:

> *I saw three ships come sailing by,*
> *Sailing by, sailing by,*
> *I saw three ships come sailing by*
> *On Christmas Day in the morning!*

"That's a dandy old carol," Wade remarked, "about ships and things. Sara, I sometimes feel that I made a mistake when I studied medicine. I'd like to be a pirate and pick you up under my arm and carry you off to unknown seas. It wouldn't hurt the children to know what it would mean to be without a mother."

❄ ❄ ❄

When Randy's new clothes came home, he tried them on and displayed himself to the assembled family. "Can you beat that?" he inquired modestly. "You've some looker for a son, Mumsie."

He *was* rather splendid, Sara told herself, with his thin grace, the fresh bloom on his cheeks, his crisp blond hair, his air of taking the world as he wanted it.

"Dance with me, Kits," he commanded, and as the two beautiful young creatures stepped in time to the music of the phonograph, Sara's heart leaped high in her breast. They were her own, and they loved her.

Yet in the darkness of the night she would sometimes ask herself, *What is love worth if it makes no sacrifices? If I should set myself against them—what then?*

Now and then she tried feebly to oppose her will to theirs, as when Kathleen, whose new dress for the party was a clear and lovely red, declared that she must have a fan to match it. "A big one. All the girls are getting them."

"Dearest, I can't afford another thing."

"You might call it my Christmas present."

"The party is my present to you, Kits."

"Mother, Uncle Wade always gives me something. Couldn't you hint to him?"

"Kathleen!"

"I don't see why you take that tone about it. And I might as well have a fan as some of those awful things men always pick out—books or workbaskets."

As it happened, Wade dropped in that very afternoon for a cup of tea. "I've been thinking," he said over the buttered muffins, "of giving Kathleen a set of books. What would she like? There's a new edition of Stevenson."

Sara poured him a fresh cup of tea before she answered. She put in three lumps of sugar and more cream than was good for him.

Then she said casually, "Do you know—I think she'd rather have something—silly."

"Silly?"

"Feminine, I mean. Like a—fan."

"Great guns! How am I going to choose it?"

She passed the plate of buttered muffins. "Would you like me to help you?"

"I would. When? Tomorrow afternoon?"

Well, they bought the fan. A beautiful thing, all waving plumes, flamingo-tinted. It was extravagantly expensive. "Oh, Wade," Sara protested when she learned the price, "you mustn't pay so much."

"Why not? Don't you like it?"

"It's lovely, of course."

"Well, then."

But Sara felt it was not well, it was ill. The cost of the fan would have fed her and the children for a week.

They couldn't keep this up. Kits *couldn't* go on having everything she wanted. They would have to stop.

At last arrived a crisis: "Mother, you can't wear that dress."

Kathleen had come home one afternoon and found her mother putting some extra touches on an old black lace. "You simply can't," she repeated.

"Why not?"

"It's so utterly out of style. And it makes you look years older."

"I have spent all the money I can possibly afford, Kathleen."

"But it will be only fifty dollars more. I saw a dress in the window—blue chiffon with silver. You'd look stunning in it, Mother."

Randy, arriving in the midst of the discussion, contributed another of his helpful remarks: "You really ought to have it. Can't you dig down in the treasure chest and find some pieces of eight?"

She told him firmly that she couldn't and wouldn't. She didn't dare think of her treasure chest, otherwise known as her safe-deposit box. The few bonds she had kept there as an anchor to windward were gone. All except for fifty dollars.

It would buy the dress. But it shouldn't. Her mind was made up. She mustn't spend another cent for nonessentials.

But Kathleen didn't look on the new gown as a nonessential. "I should think you'd *want* us to be proud of you. I should think you'd *want* to look your best. I should think you wouldn't *want* us to be—ashamed of you, Mother."

Surely the child couldn't know how those words had stabbed.

That night Wade Phillips asked Sara to go to one of the new plays with him.

Sara wore the old black lace.

"You're beautiful tonight," Wade said.

Her hands lay in her lap. They were lovely hands, slender and aristocratic. "You should have had the fan," Wade said, "only it should be blue to match your eyes."

Sara's hurt heart was comforted. At least Wade wasn't ashamed of her.

After the play they had supper at one of the best hotels. Wade ordered lobster meat under glass with mushrooms and a creamed paprika sauce, a crisp salad, and at the end, little cups of coffee. It was all delicious and Sara enjoyed it, until Wade spoke about the Christmas party. "I'm coming if I can. And I want all of your dances."

"I'm not going to dance."

"Why not?"

"I'm going to keep in the background."

"Why?"

Before she knew it she was telling him. Never before had she complained to him of the children. But now it all came out. That she had fought against having the party. That she had yielded at last against her better judgment. That to pay for it and the attendant expenses she had sold her bonds and mortgaged her income many months ahead. And that now at the very end, when she had refused to go on to other extravagances, they had said dreadful things to her.

All the time she was telling him, in the back of her mind was a sense of utter disloyalty to the family code, which had hitherto sealed her lips to outsiders, yet she wanted sympathy and expected it when she finished her story.

Wade wasted no breath in saying he was sorry for her. "Do you mean," he demanded, "that you've let them spend all that money?"

"What could I do, Wade? I wanted them to be happy."

"You could have told them to wake up and march shoulder to shoulder with you."

"I did. I tried to make them see, but they wouldn't, and now this last thing—"

She had not intended to tell him about the dress, but she did. That they wanted her to buy it with her last fifty dollars.

He gave an attentive ear: "What kind of dress?"

"Blue chiffon."

He asked a question or two after that. Where had she seen it? And what advantage would it have over the black lace? "You can't look lovelier than you do tonight, Sara. Where are their eyes?"

Going home he made up for any seeming lack of sympathy. Indeed Sara was a bit alarmed at the trend of the things he said to her. Once he laid his hand over hers, the big kind hand that had helped her over so many rough places. "You need somebody to take care of you."

❄ ❄ ❄

In the morning early, Mary Virginia came and got into Sara's bed. "Mother," she demanded, "aren't we going to have a tree?"

"Darling, we can't. We've spent all of our money for Kits's party."

Mary Virginia's voice had a disconsolate sound: "I didn't think we could have Christmas without a tree."

"Just this once, darling. Next year we'll have our tree at Solomon's Shore the way we had when you were little."

"Tell me about it."

"Me, too," said Bobby, who had arrived on the scene.

The two of them snuggled down beside their mother, rosy and bright-eyed with anticipation. "Tell us."

"Well, then, there is always snow on Solomon's Shore, so that the world is white down to the very edge of the water, and then it is blue where the waves stretch out till they meet the sky."

"And the sky is blue like sapphires," added Mary Virginia, who had heard all this before and who loved it.

"Yes. And all along the bluff above the blue sea and the blue sky are the tall spruces—"

"That stand like sentinels."

"Yes. And in between the tall trees are the little ones—"

"Just waiting to be cut for Christmas."

"Yes. And on the day before Christmas we would all go out with Daddy, and he would cut down a little tree, and we would drag it through the snow to the house and set it up by the big fireplace, and then when we were all asleep—"

"Santa Claus would come and trim it!"

"And then the very first thing in the morning we would go out and look at the Christmas star."

"Twistmas 'tar," chortled Bobby.

Mary Virginia turned on him. "You didn't see it, Bobby. You weren't there."

"Where were I?"

"Up in heaven with the stars," said the orthodox Mary Virginia.

Sara, ignoring this interlude, went on with her story: "Then we would sing 'O Little Town'!"

"Let's sing it now," said Mary Virginia.

So the three of them sang it; Sara, with her soft brown braids and parted hair making a Madonna of herself; Bobby, gold-crowned like his father; and Mary Virginia, lusty follower of the faith.

And while they sang, Sara's thoughts went back to the daddy with the gold crown and to the still white mornings down there by the sea.

"Mother," said Mary Virginia, stopping in the midst of a verse, "what are you crying about?"

"I was thinking of Daddy."

"Well, I like to think about him. It doesn't make me cry."

There was about Mary Virginia a stimulating quality. Sara felt that some day she was going to lean, not on Randy or Kathleen, but on this little daughter who had already begun to show something of her father's strength.

Bobby demanded, "Tell some more."

"Well, we went in and had breakfast and there was the tree with popcorn on it and nuts—"

"And shiny red apples and tiny wax candles."

"Yes. And after we had had our presents, old Martha

popped the turkey into the oven and we went for a walk, and when we came back—"

"We ate it all up!" They fell on her and hugged her.

Having subsided presently, Mary Virginia said: "Oh, Mother, can't we?"

"Can't we *what*?"

"Go down this year?"

"My dear, I thought you wanted Kits to have her party."

Mary Virginia had a just mind. "Well," she admitted, "I did. But I don't."

"Why not?"

"It doesn't seem like Christmas."

It didn't seem like Christmas. And it didn't seem fair to the younger children.

Sara thought about it all that day. Tomorrow was Christmas Eve, and already the house was in the process of being prepared for the party. Sara and old Martha had more than they could do. Kathleen for once proved equal to the emergency. She dusted and decorated for dear life.

It was when everything was spick-and-span, and Sara was resting from her labors, that Kathleen brought in a big box.

"Oh, Mumsie, you bought it!" she cried ecstatically.

"Bought what?"

"The dress. I opened it downstairs." She dropped the box to embrace her mother. "You darling sport, to get everything from fan to slippers."

"Fan to slippers!" Sara repeated mechanically.

Kathleen was flinging tissue paper out of the box. "You'll be a dream, dearest." She rushed into the hall and called over the stair rail, "Randy, come up and see Mother's darling dress."

He came and found his mother staring down at the chiffon gown of heavenly blue, the fan to match, the slippers.

She lifted dazed eyes. "But I didn't buy it."

"Then who?"

Sara knew. Wade had done it!

Kathleen was searching through the tissue paper for a clue. Finding none she faced her mother. "Mother, who in the world?"

Sara was white as a sheet. "I am afraid it was—Uncle Wade."

Kathleen sparkled, "How adorable! But how did he know?"

"I told him—that you didn't like me in the black lace."

She expected a thunderbolt. She had broken the family code. She had complained of them to an outsider!

But no thunderbolt came. "Of course we like you in anything!" Kathleen emphasized. "It's only that we want to be proud of you." She was radiant with satisfaction.

But Sara was not radiant. "Of course I can't keep it," she said.

"Mother!"

"My dear, if Wade sent it, it was a lovely thing for him to do. But I can't accept it. You must see that. I can't wear it, and I won't."

"Oh, gee," Randy's voice was sharp, "I should think you'd want to please us."

And Kathleen sank down on the floor beside the box and sobbed, "If you don't wear it, I'll die."

❄ ❄ ❄

Sara wore the blue dress to the party. She wore the fan and slippers. She received the guests and was a gracious and charming hostess.

When Wade came she said to him, "You shouldn't have done it. But we'll talk about that later."

She was very busy after that and only danced with him once. "I must be nice to other people," she said, "and I've got to find partners for all the wallflowers."

It was when supper was almost over that she disappeared. Wade, hunting for her, finally asked Kathleen, "Where's your mother?"

Kathleen, having the time of her life, said casually, "Oh, she's around somewhere."

But she was not around somewhere.

He went to look for Martha. But nobody had seen Martha. The caterers were packing preparatory to loading up their truck. Presently the party would be over.

And meanwhile, no Sara. No Martha.

Wade made his way to the room where the younger children slept, at the end of the apartment. They had had their refreshments early, had been tucked into bed.

The door of the children's room was shut. Wade opened it and peered in. By the low light he could see that it was empty!

Back he went through all the rooms. There was no place where the four of them could hide, Sara and Martha and Bobby and Mary Virginia. Making his worried way back to the living room, Wade found the guests leaving.

One of the caterer's men approached Wade and handed him a letter. "I was to give it to you, sir," he said, "when the evening was over."

Wade opened it and read it. He waited until the last guest had departed, then he said to Kathleen and Randy, "Your mother has gone. She left a letter."

They looked at him with startled faces. *"Gone?"*

"Yes." He read the letter to them while they sat huddled side by side on the sofa like two frightened children.

And this is what Sara had to say: "I didn't want to spoil the party, so I wore the dress. But I am enclosing a Liberty Bond for fifty dollars. It won't cover the entire cost, but I will have more for you later. And you must take it, Wade. I simply can't let you buy a dress for me, although it was dear of you to want to do it, and to try to help me.

"Tell Kathleen and Randy not to worry. The babies and I have gone to find Christmas, and we are taking Martha. Aunt Ruth sent me a check for a present and insisted that I spend it on myself, so I am spending it this way, and I'll be back when I am really rested and when I can work things out a little. I know I should have worked them out long ago, but I haven't and I make no apologies. I leaned for so many years on Daddy, and it hasn't been easy not to lean. I am afraid I haven't been a wise mother.

"That's all, and Kathleen and Randy can eat up the rest of the party, and there's money enough in my black bag in the top dresser drawer for immediate expenses."

Wade, looking up with accusing eyes, said, "You see?"

Yet in spite of his sternness he was sorry for the stricken pair. "The trouble was," he told them, "that you were thinking of your mother as a parent and not as a person. You couldn't realize that before she was a mother she was a little clinging child. Your father knew it and cherished her, and when he was taken away she had no one to cling to, and her tendrils of affection have been groping about trying to find support."

In their young eyes was dawning comprehension of a mother who needed to be shielded by their tenderness, upheld by their strength.

"We didn't know," they said.

"You might have known if you hadn't been such a stubborn pair of egotists," Wade rapped out, "but I suppose you've had to go through with it like measles and whooping cough."

Kathleen, having no fight left in her, wailed, "We can't have Christmas without her."

"No," Wade agreed, "we can't." Then, "Of course, she's gone to Solomon's Shore."

"She wanted us to go," Randy confessed disconsolately, "but Kits wouldn't give up her party."

"Randy!" Kathleen cried. "You wanted it as much as I did."

"Oh, I know. But I didn't dream . . . " His voice trailed off. Then with an effort: "When she comes back we're going to make it up to her."

"No," Wade told him, "you can't ever make it up to her. Not in the way you think. I'm going to marry her. She doesn't know it. But I do. I've been in love with her for a thousand years. And the pair of you need a father."

❄ ❄ ❄

At Solomon's Shore, before the dawn on Christmas morning, the stars shone in a sky of misty blue that was merged into a misty sea.

Sara, with Bobby and Mary Virginia, walked under that wide sky and talked in hushed tones.

"Mother, I can hear the world listening," said the imaginative Mary Virginia.

"For what, my darling?"

"For the glad tidings." Mary Virginia was walking, as it were, emotionally on tiptoe.

Sara wondered. Was the world listening? Did it care? Had the babe of Bethlehem any more than a mystical meaning to the millions who this morning would celebrate His birth?

Bobby was saying, "I want to sing."

As they turned back at last toward home, Bobby trudged along beside his mother, but Mary Virginia ran on ahead, and suddenly she stopped, and piped up alone the song that the choir had sung on the day when Sara had flung at it her bitter challenge.

> *O little flock,*
> > *What words can tell,*
> *The bliss of souls,*
> > *Christ loves so well.*

When the song was finished, the tears were running down Sara's cheeks. Oh, her little flock! How could she have dreamed of spending Christmas without all of them! Well, she wouldn't! She wouldn't!

There was a telegraph office at the little station at Solomon's Shore. The station was a squat edifice, and as Sara hurried toward it over the dunes, the light in its window shone low like another star.

"Where are we going, Mother?" Mary Virginia demanded.

"To send a telegram to Uncle Wade."

"What are you going to send it for?"

"It's a secret."

"Oh, a nice secret?"

"A lovely one."

They were satisfied with that. Christmas was a time for lovely secrets.

When they reached the house, Sara went into the kitchen, where old Martha was dishing up the children's cereal. "Martha," she said, "we're going to have six for dinner."

Martha asked, "Who-all is going to eat with you?"

Sara flushed. "I telegraphed Wade to bring the children down."

"Effen they was mine," said Martha disapprovingly, "they'd eat lean this day."

"Martha," Sara told her, "you know you're glad they're coming."

"I may be glad," Martha agreed, "but I know what's good for 'em."

Well, after breakfast Sara went out with the children, and they cut down a very small tree and brought it in and set it up, and popped corn at the fireplace and strung it in snowy chains, and hung some old ornaments on it which they found in the attic and some tiny wax candles salvaged from the same place, and some red apples that Martha had brought with her.

And it was when the turkey was all brown and beautiful in the pan, and the giblets bubbled in the rich gravy, and the mashed potatoes were in a white fluff, and the scalloped oysters plump and delectable under their buttered crumbs, that Wade Phillips's motorcar drove up to the doorway.

And Randy and Kathleen, rushing in, hugged their mother; and Wade, following them, put his hands on Sara's shoulders and said, "Did you think we'd let you spend Christmas without us?"

"That's why I telegraphed!"

They chorused, *"Telegraphed?"*

"Yes. Didn't you get it?"

"No. We started early." Then suddenly Kathleen began to cry, great tearing sobs. "Oh, Mumsie," she said, "then you *really* wanted us?"

"Wanted you?" said Sara, and they clung together.

At dinner Wade sat at the head of the table and carved the turkey. Sara sat at the foot, and she told them how they had bought everything after midnight at a market shop where the man was just turning out his lights, but turned them on again to find a turkey for them and oysters and all the other things.

And how they'd taken a late express train to the junction, and a rackety car from there; and how it was too late for Santa Claus, and they had had to trim their own tree!

Then Wade said, "It isn't too late for Santa Claus. At the very last moment he dropped a lot of boxes in my automobile."

And after they had had their mince pie, he brought them in, big boxes and little boxes, and fat boxes and thin boxes, and long boxes and short boxes, and in the boxes was everything that Bobby and Mary Virginia had ever wished for in their young lives, and a lot of things for Kits and Randy.

But there was only one box for Sara, and that was a lavender one with a bunch of violets in it, and there was a book that wasn't very new and had a bookmark in it.

And when in the afternoon Randy and Kathleen went for a walk, and the children were tucked into bed for much-needed naps, Wade and Sara sat by the fire, and outside, over the sea, the sun was going down in a burning glory, and inside there was dimness and the glow of the burning logs.

Then Wade said, "Read what I've marked in the book."

And Sara opened it and read with a shake in her voice:

> *And it's buy a bunch of violets for your lady.*
> *While the sky burns blue above. . . .*
> *On the other side of the street you'll find it*
> *shady. . . .*
> *But buy a bunch of violets for your lady. . . .*
> *And tell her she's your own true love!*

And when she finished, Wade laid his hand over her little one and said, "I've loved you for a thousand years."

And Sara, curling her fingers up to meet his own, felt her burdens fall from her, for in the grasp of that big

hand was a promise of a strength to lean on, of a
wisdom to look up to, and of a tenderness that would
follow her ranging lambs and bring them back again to
the safe shelter of the fold.

Temple (Irene) Bailey
(1869–1953)

Temple (Irene) Bailey was born in Petersburg, Virginia.
One of America's leading novelists and short story writers, she is perhaps best known for novels such as *The
Trumpeter Swan* (1920), *The Blue Window* (1926), and
short story collections such as *The Radiant Tree* (1934).

Author Unknown

A CHRISTMAS BARGAIN
IN KISSES

Things were not going well for the Young Women's Guild. Their fund-raiser was almost a complete failure. The minister's lovely daughter declared that only selling their kisses could turn the tide.

But she hadn't taken into account a certain gambler.

❄ ❄ ❄

This Canadian story is over a hundred years old. And forty dollars then was a lot of money!

❄ ❄ ❄

$\mathcal{T}$here was a flutter of expectancy as the minister's daughter came into the little back meeting room, off the main door of the church, where the members of the committee, the majority of them young and pretty, all stood talking at once.

Something was going on. In through the opening door could be heard a buzz of people, and an expert in such matters, if he had passed by and even casually looked within, would have known a church fair was in progress.

It was, indeed, the annual Christmas church fair, held under the auspices of the Young Women's Guild, and this year the minister's daughter was in charge of the proceedings. Her father, away on important business, had called her into the study before his departure and appealed to her very strongly to "do her share." And so she had announced her determination to take an active part in the preparation of the Christmas fair, much to the surprise of everyone, as up to the present time she had been more interested in playing golf, skating, and snow-shoe parties than in spiritual matters, and had even been called a "regular tomboy" by certain recalcitrant beings in old-fashioned bonnets.

"She will make a failure of it!" announced Mrs. Mintby, the official critic of the minister's family. "That girl is too harebrained, and besides, what does she know about such matters? She wouldn't be seen in church half the time if common decency didn't make her go."

"That's so," assented Mrs. Dickster. "All she cares about are the men and outdoor sports, anyhow."

And now, when the fair was half over, it began to seem as if these predictions were to be fulfilled. The booths combined had taken in barely fifty dollars, and to give a Christmas dinner to all the poor children in town—for the minister's daughter, with a fine scorn of foreign missions, had insisted that charity should begin at home—seemed a desperate chance, and at this particular moment it seemed as if nothing short of a miracle would swell the receipts for the next two hours.

The minister's daughter stepped to the table where the chairman usually presided. There was a sudden hush. She looked over her auditors a moment with a calm, penetrating gaze.

"Girls," she said, "we have got to be kissed!"

A chorus of "Oh!" and feminine screams and protests was her answer.

"There is no help for it," she continued. "We must raise a lot of money before this night is over. Now, my plan is this: We will all stand up and be kissed at auction, one at a time, to the highest bidder. Now, girls, don't go back on me. Remember, it's a good cause. How many can I count on?"

There was a pause; a hand was raised—another, and then another.

In ten minutes more eight exceedingly pretty girls, headed by one who was prettier than all of them, filed into the main room and grouped themselves about a chair. One of them stood up in the chair, to which this placard was attached:

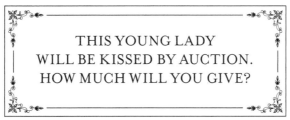

THIS YOUNG LADY
WILL BE KISSED BY AUCTION.
HOW MUCH WILL YOU GIVE?

It would probably be difficult, not to say impossible, to explain why this startling and sensational news should spread so rapidly through a whole town. But that such was the case is a stern fact. Young men idling away their time at the club knew of it in fifteen minutes and started in a body for the scene of the auction. Other young men, who had not been to church in years, hurried from their telephones into their best clothes with all the haste demanded of volunteers of a fire department.

It spread even as far as Mike Dady's gambling establishment, and caused that astute individual to prick up his ears in an unusual degree for one inured to that sort of stoicism that the roulette table fosters. And so there was a kissing game going on at the church, led by the minister's daughter herself. Here was a fine chance to get even. Mike had had to close up his place once for several weeks because of a scathing sermon preached by this same clergyman, and the remembrance of it still rankled.

"Here, boy," he said to a tall, fresh-looking youth of seventeen, handing him a roll of bills, "you go over to the church fair, and if the sky pilot's daughter is going to be kissed, push up in front and bid up. Don't let anyone else get it, to the limit of your wad—understand? I'll be there in time."

The boy, fresh and fair and innocent looking—as the run of boys in such gambling halls are apt to be—was off in a trice, and in ten minutes more had added his individual unit to the circle around the main center of public interest.

It is highly probable that if such a really scandalous proceeding as this auction had been premeditated and advertised beforehand it would have been promptly squashed by the pillars of the church. But the suddenness of it took the critics off their feet, and it was well in hand and "going on" before anyone had time to take a breath.

The minister's daughter was the auctioneer. A bamboo cane, with a strip of red bunting on it, was her wand of service. Tall and stately and beautiful, her eyes flashing with the fun, she stood by the chair and waved her flag.

"Now, ladies and gentlemen," she cried, "here is Miss Kitty Jones. How much am I offered for a sweet kiss? What! Only two dollars? For shame! Do you appreciate what you're getting? Five, did you say? Now, make it six. Six it is. Seven from the gentleman on the right. Seven, seven—eight. Eight—will someone make it nine? Nine, nine. Now, ten. That's better. Ten it is. Come, gentlemen, bid up."

The excitement ran high. Deacon Bradbury Simpkins, forgetting what fate awaited him at home, bid ten dollars on Suzie Perkins, whom his good wife had once designated as "sassy." Rodd Castleton, the best golf player in town, was a great help in "bidding up," and so also were Jack Clubberly and Billy Sparks.

The ninth and last girl was none other than the minister's daughter herself. On the table by her side lay a collection box holding over $200, the proceeds of this unusual traffic. Perhaps the consciousness that she had succeeded, that the poor, half-starved children would get at least one good square meal, was enough to make her oblivious of herself.

At any rate, she was calm and beautifully collected as she stepped on the chair, disdaining the helping hand that a spectator held out to her.

"Ladies and gentlemen," she said, "with your kind

permission I will be my own auctioneer, and I will spare you the usual compliments. I am here to raise all the money I can for a Christmas dinner for the poor children of our town. I am selling a kiss to the highest bidder. How much am I offered?"

"Twenty-five dollars."

"The first bid, ladies and gentlemen, is twenty-five dollars. Who will make it thirty? Thirty it is, thirty, thirty—thirty-five, thirty-five. Is thirty-five the highest bid?"

The tall, innocent youth now stepped to the front. It is but justice to the boys from the club to say they did not recognize him.

"I'll make it forty," he said.

The auctioneer was unmoved.

"I am offered forty dollars," she said. "Gentlemen, bid up. Forty, forty, forty—going at forty—going, going, gone. Young man, the kiss is yours at forty dollars."

There was a slight pause, a flutter of interest. This nice-looking, gentlemanly appearing boy, with forty dollars to bid for a single kiss—who was he? At any rate it didn't matter much, he was only a boy.

"What a relief," whispered one of the committee, "to think her reputation has been saved by a young thing like that. Why, it doesn't mean anything to be kissed by him. An act of Providence, I verily believe!"

Almost as if in reply the boy turned half around, as the figure of Mike Dady slowly forced its way through the circle.

"I was bidding for someone else," said the boy, holding out the money.

"Yes," said Mike, his cool, insolent eyes sweeping the crowd. "He was bidding for me. He was my—what do you call it?—proxy. I'll take the kiss, if you please."

For the first time that evening a flush spread over the face of the minister's daughter—a flush that made its way from her firmly rounded throat up over her cheeks to the line of fair hair on her forehead.

She looked around the crowd almost appealingly. Was there no one to help her in this dilemma? Suddenly her eyes lighted on a figure that stood half-concealed from view—a short, squat figure, and there came to her voice a ring of triumph.

"You shall be paid," she said. "The money, please."

It was handed to her, and she put the bills in the box.

Then she turned to the figure she had seen—the beloved old family cook, who had come to witness "the proceedings."

"Come here, Mandy," she whispered, and drawing her close and putting her arms around her, she kissed the withered face a resounding smack.

Then she turned to the gambler.

"And here," she said, "is *my* proxy. Take your pay, sir!"

Sara L. Guerin

THE SECRETARY
OF THE TREASURY PLAYS
SANTA CLAUS

The long and bloody Civil War was over at last, and the nation was all but bankrupt. After the soldiers had been paid off there was little left for all the government workers. So the sad father told his little girls there could be no Christmas for them that year.

One sister cried, and one took it bravely. At school the next day, however, she found it impossible to concentrate. Finally, she came up with a plan.

The story is true.

❄ ❄ ❄

*I*t was a bitter cold night in November 1865. The Howard family, after an early supper, was gathered around the fire, laughing and chatting for an hour before the children, two little girls, Louise and Jean, went to bed.

Mr. Howard, in the big Boston rocker, was rocking gently back and forth. There was a strained, anxious look on his pleasant face, and he answered the children's many questions in an absentminded way that was uncharacteristic.

"Now, Papa," said Louise, "that's three times you've said 'Yes, dear,' when you should have said 'No.' What is the matter—are you thinking?"

"Papa is thinking very hard, deary," said the mother. "He has a hard problem to solve."

Their father looked at the two eager faces for a moment and then said, "Come here, chicks. I'll tell you all about it."

The children sprang to him, and clasping them closely in his arms, he began. "Let me see how wise and sensible you can be. You are both almost grown-up girls now; do you think you could make a sacrifice for our sakes—Mama's and mine?"

"Oh, yes, yes! Of course we could," chorused both children. "What is it?"

"Could you two little girls give up your Christmas tree this year?"

The curly heads drooped softly to the father's shoulder. He went on: "You see, it's this way. I'm in the employment of the government—a servant of Uncle Sam. The war has been cruel and long; all the money has been used for the poor soldiers; so Uncle Sam hasn't paid me for some months, nor, I heard at the office today, will he be able to do so for some time to come. Almost all my money is used up. I dare not spend a penny for anything but food and clothes for us all; a Christmas tree and presents are out of the question. I want you both to help us bear this; for believe me, my little lassies, it's harder for us than it will be for you."

"Oh, Papa," wailed Jean, "we're too *little* to bear such dreadful things. Why, I 'most think I couldn't live without a Christmas tree! Why, we *always* have a *tree!*"

The father sighed as he kissed the tear-wet face of his darling. "What has my big girl to say?" he asked, looking at Louise. The brown curls were tossed back from the flushed face.

"Papa, don't mind Jeanie, she's too little to bear things; but I'm a big girl. Only—" here a sob was choked down—"you see we're so *used* to it, you know."

"We won't talk about it anymore tonight, as it's time to go to bed," said Mama.

As the children were going slowly up the stairs, Louise heard her father say, "If the Honorable Hugh McCulloch could know how I suffer for my children's sake tonight, he would make an effort on my behalf."

❄ ❄ ❄

Everything went wrong at school the next day. The pretty young teacher looked at Louise in amazement, for the child's thoughts seemed to be everywhere but on her lessons.

After school hours, the busy teacher looked up from her weekly reports to find Louise gazing at her intently.

"Well, dear, what is it?"

"Why, Miss Annie, I didn't say anything."

"No, dear, not with words, but you know that the eyes talk. What is the trouble?"

"I want to ask some questions. I know the owner of the United States is Uncle Sam, but what's his last name? And who is the Honorable Hugh McCulloch? And do you know where they live?"

"You funny child!" laughed Miss Graham. "I've never heard of Uncle Sam's family name, but Mr. McCulloch is an intimate friend of his—in fact, carries his purse and pays all his bills for him; and he lives in Washington."

"Oh! Well, I am going to write to him—a big letter."

"Indeed? What about, dear? Can I help you in any way?"

"You *have* helped me, Miss Annie. I think I can get it written all right. I—excuse me, but I can't tell you about it, because it's something about my father's business."

Miss Graham smiled again at the little one's dignity, but she drew the excited child to her loving arms and said, "That's quite right, my dear. Go to your desk and write your letter; I'll give you a stamp for it."

Late that afternoon the important letter was taken to the post office. Don't you think the great man must have smiled when his secretary handed him the letter, addressed in the childish writing?

This was how it looked:

HONORABLE HUGH McKULLOCH.
WASHINGTON

I think the correspondence that was carried on by the distinguished man and the little girl will tell you best how it all ended.

Nov. 30, 1865

Dear Mr. McKulloch: Won't you plese excuse me for Writing to you. I am in such trouble and want you to help me please—my papa says we can't have a chrismus tree this year, now isn't that too offley bad? He says uncle sam owes him some money and he can't get it. My papa is in the revenue business, the revenue business has stamps in it his name is mr. henry howard, 52 Sprague St. Newark N.J. won't you plese ask him to pay him else we can't have a tree, my teacher says you pay all the bills for him. wont you ask Uncle Sam to let you pay my papa? my little sister Jeanie crys all the time, she wouldent care mutch if she was ded, she feels so bad shes so littel not to have a tree. have you got any little girls. Maybe the war wouldn't let you get paid, too. I hope your little children won't have to go without any tree. Won't you plese beg uncle sam to pay up his bill to my papa plese exkuse bad speling and Writing my mamma always helps, but she don't know about this nether does my papa. Truly your littel friend,

Louise Howard
P.S. Arent you glad the war is over.

Dec. 4, 1865

My dear little friend: I was very much pleased to receive your letter. I am glad you wrote to me in your trouble, for I can and will help you.

The check for the amount the Revenue Service owes your father will be forwarded to him, without fail, by the 22d of the month—so, dear child, tell him to proceed with his arrangements for the tree. It will be all right.

I have a dear little girl like you. Her name is Louise too. She was pleased with your letter, and wishes she could have a picture of you and little Jeanie. Can you not send her one?

Yes, my little girl will have a tree too, so I am sure of the happiness of three children, at least. Wishing you and Jeanie a Merry Christmas, I am yours sincerely,

Hugh McCulloch, *Secretary of the Treasury*
P.S. *Yes, I am very glad the war is over.*

Dec. 28, 1865

Dear Mr. McCulloch: *My papa was so surprised when i got the big letter all seeling wax. he laughed and kissed me hard and said what a child but he was glad and so was mamma. I was so glad and so was Jeanie we both cryed, we thought mamma did, too—she says she dident. oh what a beautiful littel tree we had, not so Big or so fine as other years, but we liked it better, ever so much better than others because we dident expect it.*

You are such a kind Gentleman, do you see those round spots on this letter, they are kisses from Jean and me to you, this is our picture taken with the tree, do you like it, do you see that littel man hanging right in front— thats george Washington, it's a pen-wiper a littel boy in my fathers Sunday school class made it for his chrismus gift those are my skates hanging on the tabel and thats

*jeanies doll, isn't she nice. Jeanie has light hair and blue
eyes I have brown hair and gray eyes anser soon.*

Your loving friend,
Louise Howard
*P.S. I am glad you are pleased about the war being
over,—but do you know theres a dredful lot of sick
soldiers in our hospittel yet—I go and sing to them every
Saturday afternoon.*

Jan. 15, 1866

My dear little Louise: *I was more than pleased, I was
delighted, with your picture. I had it on my library table
on New Year's day, and it created great interest, and
also admiration. The tree is beautiful, but to me your
happy little faces are more so. My little Louise clapped
her hands with joy when she saw it. I enclose to you
a picture of her.*

   *I knew that was George Washington before you told
me. It is a striking likeness. I think that is a very nice
tree for hard times.*

   *I will close with many kind wishes for the new year—
indeed, for your whole future.*

Sincerely your friend,
Hugh McCulloch

That was the end—no, not quite. I think if the great
secretary could have looked into the children's room at
bedtime and seen the two little white figures kneeling at
their mother's knee, his heart would have glowed

within him; for the ending of their prayer, said in unison, was always this: "God bless Papa and Mama and Mr. Hugh McCulloch, and make Louise and Jean good girls. Amen.

Sara L. Guerin

Sara L. Guerin wrote for popular magazines during the second half of the nineteenth century.

Camilla R. Bittle

MIRACLE AT MIDNIGHT

---

*It was Christmas Eve in the hospital ward, and
Nurse Annie Hewlitt struggled against tears. Two
little boys—both earmarked for death.*

*It would take a miracle for even one of the two to
make it. . . . Unlikely though it was that such a
miracle could take place, she prayed that it might be so.*

✳ ✳ ✳

*M*iss Annie Hewlitt, head nurse on the children's ward, scanned the record and speculated about what patients were likely to be discharged by the next day—Christmas. It didn't look very hopeful. She laid the papers aside with no show of emotion, for she was not one to display her feelings. She was a big-boned, red-faced woman who had worn her cap proudly for thirty years. Sympathy flowed from her fingers, and the patients on the ward trusted her manner more readily than they accepted the glib, hollow reassurances of some of their visitors. This was certainly Miss Hewlitt's domain— doctors, nurses, and patients were her devoted subjects.

Visiting hours were over, supper trays taken up, and in a moment the house doctor would appear to go the rounds with her. Nan Kelly, student nurse, approached the desk, and Miss Hewlitt put down her papers.

"What is it, Miss Kelly?"

Miss Kelly looked uncomfortable. "It's Christmas Eve," she said.

"I know that."

"If I can get a substitute, do you think I could get off?"

"You'll have to ask the doctor." Miss Hewlitt dismissed her and watched as she went down the hall to answer a patient's ring. Nan Kelly had dark-lashed blue eyes and lovely hair. She pleased Miss Hewlitt, for she worked the way a girl works when she wants to become a nurse. Probably she wanted to go to midnight Mass with her beau, and that was a good request, Miss Hewlitt thought. The admiration of men and the spiritual serenity found in shadowed churches—these had never touched Miss Hewlitt's life. They were for the

Miss Kellys of the world, not the Miss Hewlitts, and because she knew this, Annie Hewlitt did everything she could to make the most of what she had. Her heart and soul lived right here on this ward.

The elevator doors opened, and the house doctor came up the corridor. He checked the charts at the desk and then started the rounds with Miss Hewlitt at his side. They made a good team, for they were businesslike in their approach to medicine and tender in their handling of children. As they made their way, voices rang out in laughter; parents on vigil felt encouraged, and nurses were relieved.

There were twelve patients on the ward, an assortment that included pneumonia, broken bones, and appendicitis. Sometimes the ward was free of tragedy, and Miss Hewlitt had hoped that Christmas this year would have none of it. She did not count Roger, for he represented the indisputable truth that we are all born to die. Tragedy to her was the senseless, avoidable case, and such a one had been admitted late in the afternoon. The rooms of the condemned children were opposite each other at the end of the corridor, and the only comforting thing about it was the fact that neither boy knew the Angel of Death stood beside his bed.

As they approached those two rooms Miss Hewlitt murmured, "Roger seems a little stronger."

"Sometimes an incurable will respond, but it won't last. Is he in pain?"

"Not yet."

"Well, well," the doctor said as he entered the room where a small boy lay in bed, "what's this, a Christmas tree?"

"Mrs. Thomas brought it." Roger's eyes went over the small artificial tree with its strung popcorn and homemade toy ornaments. "All the kids helped her."

Remarkable, Miss Hewlitt thought, *an orphan with thirty sisters and brothers, and a matron to mother him.* He had more real family than some of her other patients whose parents sent presents instead of coming themselves. If she were Miss Kelly, she would light a candle for Roger and pray for his immortal soul. If it assuaged the terrible ache in her heart when she looked at his thin white face and quick smile, then she would be grateful. As it was, she suffered secretly.

❄ ❄ ❄

The doctor's hands went over the slight body, gently tickled thin ribs, peered wisely into the mischievous eyes, as though he were discovering great things. The examination was only a performance, for there was no hope for Roger. All through this Roger chattered, stopping now and then, for it tired him to talk. He did not question this, but simply stopped to rest like a small animal pausing to pant.

"Who's over there?" he asked. "There's an awful lot of people in there, and about fifty nurses and doctors. Is it a boy or a girl?"

"It's a boy," Miss Hewlitt said, straightening the sheet and turning the pillow.

"What's the matter with him?" Roger asked.

"He had an accident. Now you go to sleep."

"Miss Hewlitt?"

"Yes, Roger."

"Please tell me about the boy."

Annie Hewlitt had a quick answer ready, but the look of deep concern in his face stopped her. There was so little he could take part in. Lying in bed day after day, he had lost touch with almost every part of the outside world. Now he was trying to share the activity across the hall. He wanted desperately to be a part of it. Miss Hewlitt sensed this, so she paused to explain.

"There's a boy about your age over there, Roger. He was playing with his father's gun, and he shot himself. In a little bit the doctor is going to operate and try to repair the damage."

"Gosh, does it hurt him?"

"No, he's unconscious. He doesn't know the gun went off or that he's in the hospital."

"Do you think he'll get well?"

"I hope so."

"You don't think he will, do you?"

"Oh, now, Roger. No one can tell about things like that."

"Is it Christmas Eve tonight?"

Miss Hewlitt tweaked his toe, taking mostly sheet and blanket. "That's right. Where shall we hang your stocking?"

"At the bottom of the bed," Roger said.

"Now you get to sleep or Santa won't come."

"Miss Hewlitt, about what time does Santa come?"

"Sometime in the middle of the night."

Roger's face was troubled. "Maybe I won't hang my stocking. Please, Miss Hewlitt, will you wake me up at midnight?" He pushed himself up and she went quickly to the bed, put her big, gentle hands on his shoulders and eased him back.

"Please, Miss Hewlitt. Wake me up at midnight."

"Why?"

"Mrs. Thomas told us last year that midnight on Christmas Eve was a holy time. She said that all the cows and horses in the barns kneel down because they know the baby Jesus is born and that miracles can happen."

"What miracle would you like to have happen?"

"I would like to have that boy get well."

"The doctors will do everything they can, Roger."

"But, Miss Hewlitt, his mother keeps coming out in the hall and she's crying, and so is his father, and I know he won't get well. Not without something like a miracle. *Please*, Miss Hewlitt, wake me up. I don't care about my stocking. I don't really think there's a Santa Claus anyway," he said, looking a little sheepish and rather unsure of himself.

"All right, then," she said, pulling the covers up around him and turning on the night-light. *Poor little fellow,* she thought as she left the room. *He doesn't guess that he's in need of a miracle himself.*

Miss Hewlitt glanced across the hall and saw that they had come to take the boy to the operating room. Bud was his name. Ordinary name, ordinary boy, ordinary tragedy.

At the desk, the doctor was filling out charts. He would let four go in the morning; otherwise the ward would have its full quota of Christmas patients. Miss Hewlitt saw that Miss Kelly had the doctor cornered and guessed by the smile on her face that she was getting off. Miss Hewlitt glanced at the clock. It was after nine. Another long night, and she knew it was going to be a hard one. She envied Miss Kelly as she saw her flit down the hall on her way out.

❋ ❋ ❋

Nan Kelly was glad to get off that evening. *The doctor was a doll,* she thought. *Miss Hewlitt's middle name should have been Rules. Poor dear, she probably never had anyone like Mitch waiting for her. Christmas Eve is just another night on duty to her. Well, it's not to me.* She couldn't wait to get into her "girl" clothes. Even though it was snowing, Mitch would be standing by the bench at the bus stop, a tall shadow in the yellow lamplight. Suppose she hadn't got off—she wondered how long he would stand and wait. "Forever and ever," he had said.

When she bounced down the steps of the bus into the darkness, he was there. Snow whirled around them. People pushed past them along the sidewalk, and for just a few moments she and Mitch stood with their arms around each other.

"How about some dinner?" Mitch said, tucking her mittened hand into his overcoat pocket.

"Haven't you eaten yet?"

"I waited for you."

"I know you," she said. "You're starving yourself to save money."

"Kid, I'm rich. I got a bonus. One more Christmas like this and we can get married in style."

"I don't want to get married in style. I just want to get married."

"We will. We will," he said softly. "I'll finish night

school in the spring, and then, by heaven, I'll get a job that will take care of us—including my mother."

They walked along to their favorite restaurant and ducked out of the snow into the warm smell of coffee and roasting turkey. The holly and ivy twined around the posts that set off the booths had a woodsy, Christmasy smell.

❄ ❄ ❄

For a long time they sat, drinking coffee and eating Christmas pastries. They had a great many things to talk about. It was after eleven when they went hand in hand to the church. It was nothing very new for them to go to church together. The candlelight inside shone on the graceful figures standing mute in shadowed arches— familiar friends. Still, there was something about Christmas Eve that made everything different. It was as if the saints who stood so patiently in the shadows waiting for them on this night reached out and drew them near.

As she knelt with Mitch, Nan thought about loving him. Nothing had any meaning without him. She was his friend and his playmate, and she longed to become his wife and the mother of his children. She glanced sideways at him and felt a tremble of excitement. What a father he would be to his children! Quickly she bowed her face and closed her eyes. She was ashamed to think such things in church. She prayed that she would be a good wife and mother, and as she prayed she thought about the people back at the hospital, about the boy named Bud and his parents. She remembered hearing the mother cry. As she passed up and down the hall,

Nan had heard the mother's voice tight with anger as she turned on her husband. "It was your gun," she had said. "I've begged you to get rid of it. It's your fault. If Bud dies it will be *your* fault. I'll never, never forgive you!" she had sobbed.

Kneeling in the dark church, Nan Kelly tried to pray for the child. She did pray, but she knew she could not ask for a miracle. She had seen too much of the operating room. If the miracle was not there it was not to be had. And so she prayed for his parents, because she wanted to become a good parent someday. "Father, help those poor people," she prayed. "Help them to accept Thy will and to love and comfort each other." She prayed with such feeling she could almost see the corner where they sat in the hospital.

✳ ✳ ✳

There was a waiting room on the fourth floor near the operating room, and Bud's parents had gone there when the nurses rolled the stretcher away from them. They sat in silence on the sofa, quite near each other but separated by miles of different thoughts. They had been praying ever since the gunshot rang through their house, although they didn't put their prayers into words. They didn't believe in prayer anyway. They were not people who scoffed at church and all it stood for, but they had learned to trust only the things that they could touch and control. They had worked and struggled to buy their home, hold their jobs, provide for their child. It was the only way they knew to live.

"Maybe there's a better doctor," Bud's mother said.

"Did you ask if there was another surgeon? If we paid more—a specialist or something?"

"I'm sure he's okay."

"You're sure, you're sure. How do you know? Have you ever heard of him? Why didn't you ask someone?"

"Whom was I supposed to ask?"

"How do I know?" she said frantically. "You could have called up Mr. Harris. He's your boss: He ought to know. Somebody in your club ought to know who is a good surgeon. Maybe there's somebody better."

"He wouldn't be here if he weren't all right. There are four nurses in that room and three doctors. There isn't anything else anybody can do." He moved stiffly across the leather-covered sofa toward her and reached gently for her arm. "Honey, you've got to have faith."

She jerked away from him and for the first time looked up from the floor. "Faith! How am I supposed to have faith? I knew a gun was dangerous. I told you. What's faith got to do with that? We should have locked it up or thrown it away. What difference does faith make when you know what you did wrong? Faith is for the things that are so big you don't even know what they are. I have faith the sun will come up every morning. That's what faith I have. This is different. All I want to know is that we have the best doctor there is in there."

"I'm sure he's the best there is."

"What time is it?"

He consulted his wristwatch. "Almost midnight."

"They've had him in there over two hours," she said. Suddenly she jumped up and walked across the room and stood beside the little table tree that had been set up by the nurses for visitors. The scent of spruce needles rose to her, sharp and sweet, and she closed her eyes tight. Her head bowed toward the tree, and tears rolled down her face. She had no idea that she was engaged in prayer, but she was.

❄ ❄ ❄

Miss Hewlitt found time during the evening to fill Roger's stocking. It gave her pleasure to do it. She had shopped during her time off for things that were colorful and easy to handle—little clowns that jumped on string frames, small funny animals, glass-faced puzzles. Mrs. Thomas had brought the stocking he hung every year and a box of presents from the others at the orphanage. Until tonight Miss Hewlitt had thought it would be a satisfactory Christmas, but she knew now it was nothing compared to what he wanted.

She watched the great round face of the clock on the wall. All evening she had hoped that word would come from the operating room so that at midnight when she kept her promise she could tell Roger the miracle had already occurred. She did not like to see a small boy challenge the Angel of Death with his faith. Of course, there was no other sword and shield suited to such a challenge, but she had come to love this small boy so much she felt she would die herself if he should lose his faith in such a skirmish. Without realizing it she had spent the evening in silent prayer. She didn't pray for Bud. There was no use in that. It was in the hands of the team in the operating room. Their skill was God-given and well earned, and beyond that she did not think at all. She did pray for Roger's faith. Her prayer was desperate, for she was accustomed to accepting life on its own harsh terms. Very rarely did something reach through and stir the hidden love in her, and when this happened she felt helpless. So she prayed, "Father in heaven, keep this child's faith secure. You've put Your claim on him. If he cannot have this miracle, give me the courage to keep the truth from him. Preserve his faith, for it is mother and father and home and life and love to him. It's all he has."

Miss Hewlitt laid the stocking aside. Such bumps and lumps in it—it was a ridiculous, happy thing, and she hoped it would help him for just a little while. The clock was coming around to midnight. She knew she would have to speak to him. Many times she had seen children who had caught those they trusted in a broken promise. Nothing worse could happen to a sick child.

Annie Hewlitt stood up slowly and started down the hall. She glanced once more at the clock. The second hand was sweeping up toward twelve. Gently she pushed open Roger's door. The light from the corridor fell across the bed, and she stiffened with alarm, for the bed was empty. Then she saw a tiny white form at the side of the bed, face pushed into the mattress, thin hands folded over his head. She bent down to him, and he smiled at her.

"I knew it was twelve," he said.

"Shall I put you back into bed?"

"Yes."

She lifted him up. He was like a feather in her arms. Carefully she laid him on the bed and straightened the covers. "You must have a built-in alarm clock."

Roger grinned. "It's funny—I just woke up. I haven't been out of bed for a long time, have I?" he said proudly.

"That's right, you haven't."

"I'm getting stronger, aren't I?"

"I think you are." Miss Hewlitt smoothed his forehead. It was cool, like silk on a hot day, smooth and cool. "Did you say your prayer?"

"It wasn't a prayer, exactly. You don't pray for a miracle."

"You don't?"

"No, you just believe in them."

"Will you go to sleep now?"

"Yes." He reached for her hand. "Do you suppose Santa has gone by already?" he asked wistfully.

"Goodness, no. It's snowing. He'll be around later, so you go to sleep."

Miss Hewlitt went slowly back to the desk. She would have to wait awhile before taking the filled stocking in. Even if he didn't believe in Santa, it was a pretense worth keeping. That, at least, was one miracle she could perform. The hands of the clock swung slowly.

❄ ❄ ❄

At a quarter of one the elevator light winked. Miss Hewlitt looked up from the desk, saw the white stretcher roll into the corridor and nose into Bud's room. She knew from one glance at his parents that he was going to be all right. She nodded to her old friend Betty Darkis, who came wearily up the hall, mask swinging under her chin, head wrapped in sterile gauze.

There were black rings under her eyes, but Annie knew from one look at her that she was relieved.

"Was it bad?" Annie asked.

"It was a long one."

"I didn't have much hope for him," Annie said. "You don't know how glad I am he came through."

"It's a funny thing," Betty said, sitting on the edge of the desk. "In all the time I've been in surgery I've never missed before. I could have sworn we would lose that boy. When they rolled him in he was already gone. You could *see* it. Then about midnight something seemed to happen. It was as if somebody said, 'Let's not take him after all: Let's take someone else this time.' Do you believe in miracles, Annie? Honestly, now."

Annie Hewlitt didn't answer. She had the stocking in her hand, and she was halfway down the hall, but she could still hear what Betty had said. "It was as if somebody said, 'Let's take someone else.'"

She went quietly into Roger's room, walked to his bed and reached out to him. Standing there in the darkness, she began to cry. . . .

She had known he had come to the hospital as a last stop on his journey to the inevitable, but what was the use of his miracle if he could not ride away on the glorious chariot it made?

Miss Hewlitt scolded herself, swallowed her tears, and began to do the things she had often done before. She went quietly out of the room and pulled the door shut. Then she remembered that beautiful, comical stuffed stocking. She carried it across the corridor and in her tart, crisp manner offered it to Bud's parents. "Tell him the little boy across the corridor sent it. He wanted very much for your son to have a good Christmas." With only a nod, Annie Hewlitt went on about her duties. There was a great cold lump inside her, and she wondered at the strange, bittersweet way that prayers seem to be judged.

If they had come across her desk in clear letters and figures, like the charts of her patients, she would have understood, for on that night there had been four prayers. She had prayed for a child's faith. Miss Kelly had prayed for the estate of parenthood. The parents, in turn, had prayed for their son's life. And Roger had not really prayed at all. He had simply believed . . . and it had come to pass.

Camilla R. Bittle

Camilla R. Bittle wrote both long and short fiction and nonfiction during the second half of the twentieth century.

Author Unknown

THE FORGOTTEN SANTA

He was just the school janitor—but every year for half
a century he blossomed out as Santa Claus every
Christmas. How the children loved him!

But then came the year the school board decided the
time had come to let him go.

❄ ❄ ❄

For some unaccountable reason, this story deeply
moves me every time I read it. Perhaps it's because of
what it has to say about the desire each of us has deep
in our hearts to make a difference in the short time
God entrusts to us.

*H*is name was really John Herman, and his official title had been "custodian." But everyone in town knew him as "Hermie" the janitor. No one knew just how old Hermie was, but some of the older people in town could recall that he had taken care of the grade school when they were pupils there—half a century before.

Hermie had no family. He had never married, and no one knew just where he had spent his early life. His only home was a small room in the basement of the school. When asked why he didn't get himself a better place to live, Hermie always answered with a chuckle, "Well, you see, it's like this: That big, old furnace in the schoolhouse is kinda like a spoiled child—it needs watchin'. As long as I'm right there with it, there's no chance of it actin' up." And truly, Hermie babied the enormous furnace that heated steam for the classroom radiators like it was a child. At times, he had even been overheard talking to it like it was another human being.

In spite of the menial aspect of his job, once a year Hermie had his day. Every year on the Friday before Christmas the school would celebrate with a party and a Christmas tree, attended by scholars, their parents, and the young fry. Only one man had the build to portray jolly old St. Nicholas. And so each year, as the last and happiest event on the happy program, there would emerge from the furnace room—as though he had descended the chimney of the furnace itself—a vision of Santa Claus that delighted young and old alike. Laughing through a surefire routine perfected by years of practice, Hermie would captivate the youngsters, holding little boys and girls on his knee, whispering surprises in their ears, and carrying out his act with complete authenticity, even to the hearty laughter and the twinkling eye.

Finally—only after the principal had given him several unobtrusive, insistent nods—old Santa would reluctantly bid each one good-bye, and waving merrily and calling "Merry Christmas to all!" he vanished through the doorway of the old furnace room. But so realistic had been his portrayal that some of the youngest ones would have insisted he disappeared "up the chimney."

After the holidays, when school resumed, Hermie would be there sweeping up, the same trudging old man—just the janitor who lived in the basement—no resemblance at all to the jolly Christmas visitor, unless one looked deep into the faded blue eyes where lingered the same twinkle that children loved so much.

But the years took their toll, and one spring day the school board decided that Hermie was no longer able to stoke the huge furnace and sweep the long corridors, so they retired him on a pension. At the end of the school year, Hermie gathered together the few personal possessions he had accumulated through the years and packed them into several small boxes. He made one last thorough sweeping of the classrooms and corridors, tidied up the small basement room he'd called home, and shined and polished the huge front door of the old furnace till it gleamed. Then, giving it a gentle pat as though bidding good-bye to an old friend, he trudged out of the school for the last time.

Hermie found a tiny house on the edge of town that no one had occupied for a long time. It would not be as warm as the school basement, but it was "a roof over his head" anyway, and the rent was cheap.

During the summer months and into the fall, Hermie puttered and puffed at odd jobs around town, trying to keep busy. After the first snow of the winter, he took to the house and was not seen again for several weeks. But if anyone happened to miss seeing him, no one took the time to see how he was doing.

The Friday before Christmas was a cold, brisk day. A light snow had fallen the night before, covering the ground and bushes with a fluffy white blanket. Classes had just taken up in the school when Miss Oliver, the principal, glanced out of the window and saw a familiar figure trudging up the front walk carrying a large suit box. A look of dismay crossed Miss Oliver's face as she realized the old man's mission. In a moment the door of the office opened, and Hermie entered quietly.

"I thought you might be needin' a good Santy Claus, Miss Oliver," Hermie said, smiling broadly.

The principal bit her lip and looked helplessly at the old man. Finally she said, rather huskily, as though to have it done with, "I'm sorry, Hermie—we've already got a man." The old man nodded and hung his head. "But here," added Miss Oliver, "the school has a Christmas present for you." She handed him a large box of chocolates that someone had given her. The old man took it hesitantly, mumbled a few words of thanks, and slowly turned and left the office.

From the school Hermie went to the churches, one at a time, and then to several of the businessmen in the town, seeking a one-night stand in his favorite role. Each place it was the same—but each place the minister, or businessman, or someone, was moved by the pathetic gesture of the old man who hated to lay aside his seasonal masquerade. The best they could do was a gift, and he got all kinds, all of them last-minute items. One of the businessmen gave him a pair of too-small gloves, another's wife donated a hand-knit wool scarf, and so on. He went home loaded with "presents"; and back at the cottage he found a basket from a welfare group and a turkey donated by the local service club. By Christmas Eve, his table was overflowing.

Dusk was just descending on Christmas Eve when a familiar figure emerged from the tiny house on the edge of town. If the once bright red suit was now a bit faded and streaked, and if the once snowy white beard was speckled with flecks of coal dust—no one would have noticed. The twinkling eyes and the sprightly step were undoubtedly those of Santa Claus. And he might have been heard to chuckle merrily as he shifted his familiar pack from one shoulder to the other. And in the dim light of the evening, the large gunnysack filled with charitable "presents" was transformed into a magic pack laden with gifts.

Happily the jolly fellow tramped through the snow from one lowly house to another, visiting the poorest homes he could find, distributing his gifts. At each place where there were children, he would stop to tell them about his reindeer and the North Pole. He made many stops, for in addition to the gifts he had received, he had included such things as a set of sterling silver teaspoons that had belonged to his mother and several books he had treasured for many years.

It was nearly midnight when the tired old man returned to his cottage, his empty gunnysack dragging behind him. If anyone had been watching, they would have seen a dim light burning for a short time and then going out, leaving the tiny cottage in complete darkness.

Through the busy holidays no one thought about Hermie or missed him. One day several weeks later, one of the ministers decided to stop by the cottage. And there he found Hermie lying in a peaceful sleep, a sweetly reminiscent smile on his careworn face.

Later, when neighbors came in to sort through Hermie's belongings, they found practically nothing but several empty boxes—and neatly folded on a chair in the corner a worn Santa Claus suit.

Albert Payson Terhune

THE YULE MIRACLE

A collie pup that turned out to be silly and worthless was given to fifteen-year-old Karen Brayle one Christmas. The following Christmas, her father offered to take the dog off her hands.

But there was something about the dog she had never told her family.

❉ ❉ ❉

*J*t was a pretty trick that Karen Brayle had taught her Christmas collie. She and the dog had happened upon the game by accident. Thereafter, they played it a hundred times when they were alone together.

Indeed, it was almost the only thing she or anyone else had ever been able to teach the big, lumbering young dog. So Karen was the prouder of it. But, always fearing the puppy would get stage fright and humiliate her if she should attempt to play it with him in public, she contented herself with private performances.

Nor did she brag of the collie's single achievement, lest incredulous hearers insist on her proving its truth and lest the dog add to his unpopularity in the family by flunking the test.

On the Christmas Eve before, Mr. Brayle had brought home the huge, leggy young dog as a Yule gift to his only daughter. Karen had been rapturously happy over the present. In memory of the day, she had named her gift "Yule"; a short and easy name to call him by, but a name to which he did not respond unless he felt inclined to.

The young collie had been beautiful in golden coat and unduly large in bone. The deep-set, dark eyes should have held a blend of mischievousness and stern-ness. Instead, the expression was merely foolish. Yes, that was the keynote of Yule's nature. He seemed incur-ably foolish.

Karen found this out before he had been in the house a day. So did the entire Brayle family—Karen's father and mother and her two older brothers. One and all, they had read and had heard of the uncannily keen brain power of collies, of the breed's loyalty and chumship. Great things had they expected from this overgrown pedigreed pup. And not a thing did they get.

It was as though people had paid a stiff price to see the tragedy of *Hamlet* and had found a slapstick film substituted for the Shakespeare play, or had gone to an Einstein lecture and been confronted by the village idiot.

Nothing did the bumble-puppy collie know, and nothing did he seem able to learn. The more they worked with him, the duller he seemed to become. He had a genius for getting into the house and ripping rugs to rags and disemboweling overstuffed chairs and yanking down window curtains. But he could not be taught to obey or even to answer to his name.

He was a pest, a nuisance, a dead loss.

At first the Brayles were dazed with incredulous surprise at the silliness of the collie from which they had hoped so much. Then they piled derisively disgusted epithets on him and accepted Yule as a mighty bad joke on themselves.

All but Karen.

Even as a mother often feels more tenderness for some crippled or dull child than for her normal offspring, so the sneering ridicule of her parents and brothers made Karen cling more lovingly to poor, brainless Yule.

This although she knew better than anyone else how utterly worthless the dog was. It was she, for instance, who undertook to train him and who plumbed the total lack of his intelligence to its depths. It was she who, on one of their first walks together, witnessed the humiliating scene when a miniature-size Pomeranian growled at the shambling golden giant and Yule fled howling under the nearest porch at the tiny lapdog's attack.

"No brains," mused Karen. "No courage. No affection. Nothing but bigness and appetite. That's you, poor Yule."

The dog thumped his tail on the floor as she spoke. She thrilled in hope it meant he recognized his name at last. But he was only wagging his plumed tail because he saw the cook drawing near with his basinful of dinner scraps. Almost fiercely, Karen threw her arms around the shaggy neck and hugged the vacuously grinning Yule to her heart.

"Never mind!" she consoled him—though he stood in scant need of consolation and was far more interested in the approaching dinner basin than in his young owner. "Never mind, Yule! I love you better than I love anyone else except the family. I don't know why, but I do. You can be as stupid as you like. I'll keep on loving you, just the same—"

She broke off in her crooned whisper of comfort, because Yule tore loose from her arms and went charging clumsily at the basin the cook was carrying to him. Karen left him in disgust. In spite of the care she had spent on him, the poor puppy seemed as hopelessly silly as ever.

It was during the first warm week of spring that Karen discovered the dog's only trick, the one I have spoken of. By that time, the girl was the sole member of the household who would so much as glance at Yule, much less speak to him. The rest were thoroughly disgusted with him. But for Karen's affection for the uncouth creature, he would have been packed off long before.

By the time the winter ice broke up in the lake a furlong from the Brayle home, Karen had taken Yule to the water to teach him to swim. To her disappointment, though not to her surprise, the collie refused to go into the lake any farther than his own midlegs. There, before the water could reach as high as his stomach, he would recoil, tail between legs, and run *ki-yi*-ing to the shore. (This, by the way, was not necessarily a part of his normal cowardly idiocy. Not one collie in five enjoys swimming or will go voluntarily out of his depth in water. But not one collie in ninety will *ki-yi* or show other abject signs of terror when he is urged into the deeps.)

The first day of the season when she was allowed to go swimming, Karen ran down the beach with Yule capering and barking alongside. When she was ankle-deep in the lake, she stumbled. Seeking to right herself, she lurched sidewise and fell prone on her face in a few inches of water.

Instantly, Yule's fanfare of barking swelled tenfold. He charged over to the prostrate girl. Seizing her by one shoulder of her bathing suit, he dug his teeth deep into the cloth and braced his four feet, hauling backward with all his strength to drag her to land.

Karen was overjoyed at this manifestation of the life-saving instinct. She praised Yule loudly and effusively, patting and lauding him until he danced in ungainly pride.

Twice more, in succession, the girl ran down the beach and fell sidewise into the shallow water. Each time Yule rushed barking after her and sought to haul her ashore. Each time he was praised as fulsomely as at first. He waxed vastly proud of himself, vanity being the one salient collie trait he had thus far developed.

Then came the real test, a test that Karen approached without a qualm of misgiving, a test that would give her something to boast of at home and that could not fail to boost Yule's stock with the whole disapproving family.

She dashed down the beach afresh. But this time she did not fall prostrate in eight inches of water. Instead, she kept on, until she could no longer feel the lake pebbles under her feet. Then, throwing herself on one side, she began to flounder and to call to Yule for help.

As a matter of fact, Karen was about as much in danger of drowning as would be a duck that is tossed into a pond. Almost from babyhood she had been an expert swimmer. But she gave a really creditable imitation of a drowning person. All the while, she watched with one eye the big golden collie on the beach behind her.

Let Yule once plunge into the lake and swim out to her and catch her by the shoulder and try to pull her ashore, and she would know he had the true collie soul, the clean white heart that will risk death to save a loved human being. Eagerly she waited, redoubling her splashing and her calls for help.

Yule raced up and down the bank, barking in asinine futility, once or twice venturing out into perhaps twelve inches of water and then shrinking back to shore to recommence his deafening idiotic barks. He was giving a magnificent exhibition of panic-stricken uselessness, and his every movement showed he lacked any of the pluck needed to go to his supposedly drowning mistress's rescue.

Disillusioned, cruelly chagrined, Karen swam shoreward and climbed the beach. Yule met her ecstatically, as though congratulating her on her lucky escape from death. For a moment she glared angrily down upon the capering dog. Then she stopped and patted him.

"Poor, worthless Yule!" she exclaimed, with more tenderness than contempt in her voice. "You can't help being what you are. None of us can. And perhaps somewhere there are collies like the ones in the stories. It isn't your fault you're not one of them. I love you, anyhow, if nobody else does."

Daily, after that, at the outset of her swim, Karen and Yule went through that mock lifesaving stunt, in water eight inches deep. The sport never palled on the young dog. Indeed he became more and more dexterous at it, learning to take better grip and to use wiser leverage.

But ever when Karen swam out into the lake, the collie remained timorously behind. Try as she would, Karen could not coax him into deep water. When she pretended to be in distress, he would bark plangently and run up and down the beach. But not once did he venture out to her aid. In short, he was an ideal life-saver, as long as he could enact the role without getting wet or risking a swim.

Karen loved him for what he was, not for what she had hoped he might be. Nobody else loved him at all. None of the Brayles could endure the sight of the clumsy clown collie. Karen endured much teasing from her brothers and many a sour look from her father because of her silly golden comrade.

❆ ❆ ❆

The long summer drowsed away. Autumn brought V-shaped cohorts of wild geese flying southward across the lake. Winter set in.

Karen and Yule had been inseparable comrades till the girl went to school that fall. But Karen had given up trying to ding sense into the collie's thick head. She accepted him for a stupid and bumptious and beautiful plaything.

Meanwhile, the passing year had brought depth to Yule's chest and grace to his limbs and a massiveness to his heavy gold and white coat. Ignorant of collies, the Brayles scarcely noted these very gradual physical changes, nor did they bother to guess whether or not age was working similar development to the dog's soul and brain.

The fox terrier puppy at six months old is graceful and fleet. The lion cub, at the same age, is gawkily helpless. Thackeray was a giant. As a boy he was rated a lazy fool. Bismarck was a giant. As a boy, he could not so much as master his lessons and later was dropped from college. The boy Lincoln was shambling and physically lazy.

But if the Brayles had heard of these cases of the slow development of giants, they most assuredly did not apply the rule to the gigantic collie they despised.

❆ ❆ ❆

Christmas was drawing near. There was no more promise of a white and icy Christmas that year than that Yule would turn into a prodigy. The dank chill of November continued to hang over the land, without merging into the tingling cold of late December.

As a general thing, long before Christmas, the lake was several inches thick in glass-clear ice and the hills were glittering with deep snow. But now the ice merely formed in a skim along the shore. The land lay glumly gray-brown and snowless. There could scarcely have been less appropriate Christmastide weather or scenery.

Karen came home for the holidays to be greeted rapturously and loudly by Yule. For her sake the collie had been tolerated during her absence.

The morning after her return, her father called her into his study. He and she were alone in the house at the moment, except for the collie, which Mr. Brayle shoved impatiently from the room as Yule strove to follow Karen in.

"Listen, daughter," began Mr. Brayle, without preamble. "All of us want you to be happy. You know that. We want you to have the very happiest Christmas we can give you. But . . ."

"But what, Daddy?" asked Karen, puzzled.

"But that's just what we tried to do for you last year," pursued her father. "That's why we bought Yule for you. And look how he's turned out! I'd call him an unmitigated nuisance if I weren't afraid of doing rank injustice to some *real* unmitigated nuisance. That's what I want to talk to you about this morning."

"But I love Yule," protested Karen. "He and I—"

"You mean you love all animals. Yule is the only animal you've ever played around with, so you think you're fond of him," corrected Mr. Brayle. "Now here is my idea. For one solid year we've put up with that fool dog. We have been the laughingstock of the people on both sides of us. He hasn't a scrap of intelligence or of loyalty or of companionableness. He's a one million percent failure. He—"

"But I—"

"Wait a minute. I know a man who will take him off our hands. He says he'll give him a good home in the city. He lives alone in a flat there, and he wants some companion to welcome him home at night. I didn't tell the man quite what a fool the collie is. He'll find that out soon enough. But I told him I'd try to get you to consent to part with Yule. If you will, daughter, I've a chance to buy you a splendid well-trained clever Boston terrier in his place. The Boston can be delivered here Christmas morning. It's up to you. What do you say?"

For a long half minute, Karen Brayle faced her father. She felt she was growing red and redder, and an unbidden mist began to creep in front of her unhappy eyes. Patiently, Mr. Brayle waited for her to speak. He seemed relieved to have said his say. At last Karen spoke. Fast she spoke, and with growing speed and incoherence.

"I love Yule," she repeated. "And he loves me. I know that. But even if I didn't care anything about him, I'd rather see him shot than sent to a little flat in a big city. He'd have to spend the whole day in a space no bigger than our porch here all alone and wondering why I deserted him."

Despite her self-control, something had risen in her throat that threatened to choke her. Now, lest she disgrace her sixteen years of age by tears, Karen turned abruptly and fled from the room. Mr. Brayle watched with worried face as he saw her run out of the house and along the sloping hillside below.

Mr. Brayle sighed, and was about to turn away when his gaze focused on the girl.

In her aimless craving to be alone, Karen Brayle had unconsciously taken the hillside path that led down to the lake edge to the pier, which jutted out into deep water. Out onto the ice-slippery pier she made her blind way. At its stringpiece, she checked her haste. At least, she tried to. It was then that her father's idly sympathetic gaze turned sharp and worried.

Karen's smooth-soled house shoes slid along a swath of ice that had formed.

She strove vainly for her balance, lurched forward, her feet going out suddenly from under her—and slid off the edge of the string-piece and down into twelve feet of ice-strewn water.

Mr. Brayle shouted in impotent terror. Bursting out of the house, he ran down the slope at blundering speed. Not that he feared Karen would drown, despite her thick clothing, but lest the wintry ducking give her pneumonia. Immersion in such icy water, followed by a buffeting from the cold morning wind, might well make her gravely ill.

Mr. Brayle himself had never bothered to learn to swim. He had envied his daughter her skill in the water. But he'd not envied her enough to learn the same art. He was running down to the pier simply that he might wrap her in his heavy dressing gown when she should emerge.

Then his pace quickened, and his face went rigid.

For, as Karen struck out, he saw her double up and claw helplessly at the water with constricted fingers.

Nervous excitement and the dive into the bitterly cold water had sent a cramp through every inch of her athletic body. Her legs and arms contracted in anguish.

Mr. Brayle yelled for help as he ran. But he knew how useless the shout was. His wife and sons had driven to the nearby village. There was no human being within a mile.

Then, whizzing past him like a flung spear, something big and golden dashed at express train speed toward the lake.

Onto the pier flew Yule. At the string-piece, the collie launched himself outward, with no shadow of hesitation, into space. His shaggy body smote the water, not a yard from the sinking girl, and immediately his mighty jaws seized the shoulder of her stout sweater.

Then, heading instinctively toward the strip of beach below the pier, Yule towed the knotted and impotent girl toward shore. Inch by inch the dog beat his way shoreward, tugging with him the adored mistress whom so often he had hauled playfully along in shallow water.

Karen's feet grated against the pebbles of the shoal. Her father rushed out, knee deep into the chill water, and snatched her in his arms. In only seconds he had wrapped Karen in his thick dressing gown and was running as fast as he possibly could with her toward the house. Yule loped easily after them.

An hour later, after a vigorous rubdown with a crash towel and a still more vigorous alcohol rub, Karen sat in a big chair in her father's study, her feet to the fire, her parents and brothers gathering about her.

In the midst of her oft-repeated story of the rescue, Yule walked into the room. Majestically, he strode up to his young mistress and laid his classic head on her knee.

A moment's silence fell upon the group. All of them were staring dumbly at the huge collie. It was Mr. Brayle who spoke.

"Look!" he bade the rest. "Look at those eyes! What has become of their flat silliness? See! The true 'look of eagles' is lurking behind them. He's—he's a *dog*! Not a clown anymore."

"It was there all the time," said Karen, gathering the splendid head tightly into her embrace. "More and more it was there. But something had to be worn away by time or else snatched away by a shock, to change him from a big puppy to a great dog. It's *happened*. Do you still want to swap him for a terrier, Daddy?" she added mischievously.

Mr. Brayle shuddered. Slowly he crossed to where Yule stood close beside Karen's deep chair. Half-hesitantly the man held out one hand, as if in propitiation.

"Yule," he said humbly, "I apologize. No other dog is ever going to replace you here, as long as I live. Will you shake on it?"

Gravely, with an air of perfect equality, Yule laid one white forepaw into the man's outstretched palm.

"We've got a Christmas collie at last," remarked Mr. Brayle, his other hand lying on the dog's silken head. "A perfect Christmas collie. One year behind schedule."

Albert Payson Terhune
(1872–1942)

Albert Payson Terhune was born in Newark, New Jersey. During his long publishing career, Terhune specialized in stories and novels with dogs as their central characters. Among the most popular are *Lad, a Dog* (1919), *Wolf* (1924), and *The Book of Sunnybank* (1935).

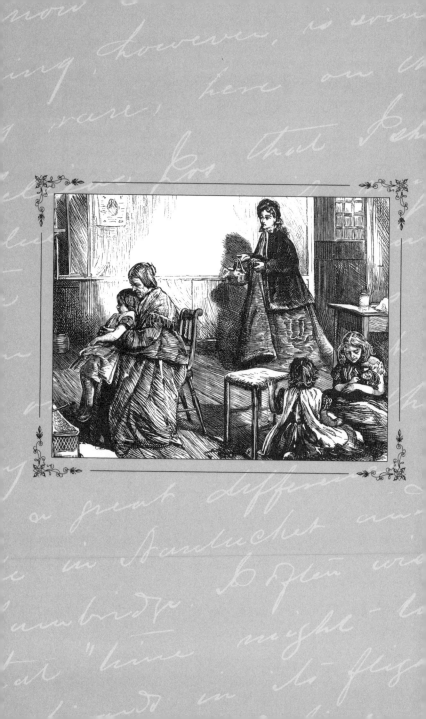

Christie Lund Coles

THE WHEELCHAIR

Eulalie Thompson had everything that money could buy. What she didn't have was what a wan seventeen-year-old invalid had. On a whim, she decided to go over and meet her.

❇ ❇ ❇

*E*ulalie Thompson stirred from her position on the floor of the gaily decorated nursery and lifted red-rimmed eyes to her husband, Dr. Jerry Thompson, as he entered, looking a little tired and a little drawn.

"H'lo."

She didn't answer but slowly began putting little shoes, soft knit sweaters and hoods, broken bits of toys, and countless other things into a large white wicker chest—belongings of a small boy who had laughed and romped through this cheerful room, until . . . An expensive wheelchair sat in one corner of the room.

"It's four years ago today that he died; and to think that he was a prisoner of that horrid wheelchair for over a year."

"Well, why don't you get rid of it if it has such unpleasant memories for you?"

"Oh, Jerry, how could I when it reminds me of him?"

"But I want you to bear up. You can't go on this way. You can't grieve forever. I want you to remember the happiness of his life. Think of the eight years of unbounded health before he went. Life can still mean so much. Think of all the things you have. You should be uptown shopping, seeing the crowds, buying gifts."

"Who for?"

"Haven't you dozens of friends?"

"Yes, but what could I give any of them? Who is there I could make happy?"

"You could make yourself happy if you would try. I've learned that one has to go on. One has to buck up no matter what the odds are. We're not the first nor the millionth to know grief—can't you see? Why there's that little Anderson girl up there in that dark tenement—she's never taken a step in her life—not one step, and yet she's happy and so is her mother, though there are five other youngsters to feed and clothe and worry over."

"Why couldn't she die?"

"Oh, but Lilyce isn't a misery to anyone—so sweet and uncomplaining. Why don't you go and see her some day? There are so few who come."

"I don't want to go anywhere."

The doctor left to visit his patients. Now the house was like a tomb, an unbearable tomb. There would be no Christmas tree this year—no little wagon and horn and sleigh—nothing. Oh, she couldn't bear it! She slipped on a magnificent fur coat. Pulling a small hat over her blond hair, she almost ran out of the house. She didn't know where she was going; it didn't matter—anywhere to get away from the memories of this house. On a sudden impulse she decided to go to that little girl Jerry had spoken of so often—she would understand what Junior had suffered. And dear Jerry, he was always making sacrifices in his work. Half the time, the cases were charity cases like this.

When she had climbed the three flights of narrow stairs, she was out of breath. After all, what right had she to be there? What excuse could she give for intruding?

Before she could retreat, someone opened the door. Mrs. Anderson was there, wiping the perspiration from her brow with the corner of her apron.

"How do you do?" said Mrs. Anderson.

"Good morning. I'm Mrs. Thompson, Dr. Thompson's wife. I came to see the little girl who is ill. My husband has spoken of her so often."

"Well, if it isn't just like the doctor to send you up. He's the finest man God ever saw fit to set on two feet. We're proud to have his wife visit us, though you came on a mighty busy day; with Christmas baking and such, it keeps a body rushing. Come right in where Lilyce is. She'll be glad to see you."

She was taken to the dining room, and there she saw a bed that was located by the only window in the room, where the view was a tall gray building with a small patch of sky on one side. Lilyce was a white-faced girl of seventeen. Her face was pale and drawn, her eyes were too large and too bright. Five other children were seated on the floor near the bed playing.

"You see," said Lilyce, "we keep my bed here because it's lighter and warmer and then I can be with the folks."

"It must be hard," Eulalie murmured, "hard to lie here, day after day."

"No, it isn't hard—it's much easier than you might think. I live in a world of my own where there isn't any jangling or disappointment. If the day is dark and I get lonesome, I close my eyes and I'm in a place where the sun is shining—California, maybe, and I'm a movie queen, dressing in swell clothes and going out to dinner. Then again, I may play that I am married to someone nice and kind like Dr. Thompson, and we're living in a little white house, with roses, the rambling roses, and there are little babies to play with and scold and make cookies for. I think that is my favorite dream."

"How *wonderful* . . . you like Dr. Thompson?"

"Oh, yes, he is always so patient and kind: I think I could stand all the pain in the world if he were there:

The minute he comes into the room I just feel better. And then there are other dreams. I've never seen a rose—but I just know how wonderful they are. Patty tells me about all the flowers in the park and those in the windows uptown; and isn't it wonderful that people can have them?—that is, *some people*."

Eulalie thought of the hundreds of roses that had bloomed and died, unpicked, practically unnoticed, in the spacious gardens back of her home.

After a while, Eulalie went into the kitchen with Mrs. Anderson.

"My, how good your Christmas cooking smells!"

"Does it? Well, we try to get enough to eat once a year anyway. Won't you taste my pie?" And without giving her a chance to refuse, she had set a huge piece before her.

"Sit down and eat it, and you *must* taste my fruit-cake."

Eulalie found it pleasant to be there eating pie—it took her back again to her grandmother's kitchen.

"Your daughter is wonderful, so very happy and patient."

"Why, I don't know what we would do without her. The whole family just lives around her. She reads everything she can lay her hands on. If we quarrel, she quotes something beautiful to us and makes us ashamed of ourselves."

"You've had six children?"

"No, ma'am, I've had nine; three of 'ems dead."

"Three of them, three children *died*? Not really? Oh, how terrible it must have been to lose them!"

"Well, it was hard at the time, but we have the

consolation of knowing they're safe. It's the living ones that need our pity and love."

Eulalie rose and patted the head of the boy who had just come into the kitchen.

"Well, what's Santa going to bring you, sonny?"

"Nothing."

"Nothing?"

"Nope . . . Can you keep a secret? None of us are going to get anything. Mama and Pop are going to take all the money they've saved up for presents and shoot the works on a wheelchair for Lilyce. Gee, lady, just think! She ain't seen the park or nothin', and when she gets that we can take her out every day. Won't that be swell? Gee whiz! Jes' think—a real big wheelchair. An' I'm going to push it, too; she said I could."

"But isn't there anything you would like for Christmas?"

"Naw, why, when she's in bed, us kids can push each other around in it and play train. That would be fun!"

Eulalie returned to the girl who had never seen a rose, never seen a sunset, never known anything but this little room and two withered legs.

"I really must be going. I've stayed much longer than I had planned."

Mrs. Anderson followed her to the door. "I'm right sorry things have been in such confusion, but I do hope you'll come again soon."

"It was marvelous, marvelous! And now I want you to let me help you play Santa Claus to these children. I have been very selfish, and consequently very unhappy. I have a lovely wheelchair, one that I know Lilyce would like, and I want you to take it for her. I'm going to send up some other things to prove to these children that such beautiful unselfishness is worthwhile."

The older woman was wiping her eyes on the corner of her apron.

"I always said—if we do what's right, the Lord will open the way. I know it's not much, but we'd love to have you and the doctor come for supper and spend the evening. We have a nice time playing games and singing—that is, if you haven't planned something else."

"Oh, we'd love to!" and in a moment she was hurrying down the steps, carrying with her the echoes of a dozen "Merry Christmases."

She hurried uptown and burst into Jerry's office.

"Merry Christmas, Jerry!"

"Why, honey, and the merriest to you!"

"Hurry, dear! I want you to do some shopping with me. I'll explain later."

Christie Lund Coles

Christie Lund Coles wrote during the first half of the twentieth century.

Torey Hayden

CARLA'S GIFT

Seventy-three children in the school, all with behavioral disorders of one kind or another; a number with low IQs. One of them was Carla.

When asked what she wanted most for Christmas, she answered, "Red . . . red, red, red. Balloon. Birthday balloon."

Since nothing else would do, the teacher decided to humor her.

But it wasn't enough.

✳ ✳ ✳

A true story.

*Y*ou almost didn't notice her in class. She was small for seven, and quiet; she didn't cause trouble the way the boys did. Her features were plain, and her blond hair was cropped short in a raggedy, home-cut style vaguely reminiscent of the Little Prince. No matter what the time of year, she always wore the same assortment of faded cotton dresses, the same cheap sneakers. Her name was Carla.

My specialty was behavioral disorders, although my class that year wasn't a traditional class for emotionally disturbed youngsters. Most of my seven students—six boys and Carla—were simply victims of abject poverty.

All seventy-three youngsters in the old sandstone school building were in special education. The floor below me housed two preschool programs. Our floor had a class for mentally handicapped six- to nine-year-olds taught by my colleague, Maia, and my own class.

Carla should have been in with Maia. The tests administered in kindergarten gave Carla an IQ of 69—our school district rated any score below 70 as indicative of a mental handicap. But I had fewer students than Maia did, and Carla had a speech problem. By virtue of my interest in psychologically based language difficulties, I had become the school's unofficial speech expert.

Carla's talents were not many. She couldn't read. She was hopeless at art. She couldn't even stick the ends of paper strips together to make chains. And the simplest math activities defeated her.

"Here, see what I have here?" I said to her one morning, and laid out twelve wooden cubes. "Can you count these?"

"One, one, one . . ." she struggled.

I put a hand over hers and moved it along as I counted. "One, two, three . . ."

"Four, five, six," she continued alone, "seven, nine, ten, eleven . . ."

"Whoops, Carla, you left out eight. One, two . . ."

"Three, four, five, six, seven, nine . . ."

"Whoops, you've left out eight again. Here. Do it with me." I covered her hand and moved it along the cubes.

"One, two, three, four, five, six, seven, eight, nine, ten, eleven, twelve. What comes after seven?"

"Eight," she said. "Eight, eight, eight."

"Good. Now you try it by yourself."

Carla hesitated and then began. "One, two, three, four, five, six, seven, *eight*, ten, eleven, twelve!"

"Whoops, Carla, you've left out nine. . . ."

I tried to be understanding, but I didn't have Maia's patience working with such a slow student. With the boys clamoring for attention—their minds lively, if not sharp—I sometimes resented the time Carla required to learn something. I knew however much time I put in, I wouldn't get much out of her. Carla just didn't have much to give.

✳ ✳ ✳

Christmas was a big event in our school. Because so many children came from poor families, many homes would have no tree and few presents. And with so many broken families, no festive gatherings.

We attempted to catch the best of the holiday spirit at school. We tried to emphasize simple pleasures—that there is more to Christmas (even to the secularized version we celebrated in school) than the gaudy commercialism presented on television. This inspired a good deal of creativity as we, too, were on a very limited budget.

One of the service clubs in town provided us with a large Christmas tree, which we erected in the gym and decorated with sugar cookies. Another provided a Santa Claus and a sackful of toys for our party on the last day before the Christmas vacation. The members collected secondhand toys every year and renovated them, so the gifts given out during the party were nice and, for many of the children, would likely be the only toys they received. As a consequence, we on the staff did our best to match the toys with appropriate children. The best way we found was to have the kids write letters to Santa.

My group, of course, was enthusiastic when letter-writing time came around. Mikey, a rather streetwise six-year-old, snatched up his paper. "I know what I'm going to ask for. One of them four-wheel dirt bikes."

"That's too big for Santa to bring, don't you think, Mikey?" I asked. "He only has one sack to hold all the gifts. I doubt a dirt bike would fit."

"Santa Claus is just a big fake-o anyway," Nathan announced. Nathan was eight and worldly.

I sat down beside Carla, who was having trouble copying "Dear Santa" from the blackboard. "What do you hope Santa brings you?" I asked.

"Red," she said. "Red, red, red. Balloon. Birthday balloon."

"A balloon?"

"Red balloon. Go up, up, up."

"A balloon?" Nathan shouted. "You want just a balloon for Christmas? What a stupid idea!"

"Nathan! Shush!" I said to him.

"Birthday balloon," Carla said. "Christmas Jesus' birthday."

"Yes, it is. That's why we celebrate Christmas, isn't it? But what would you like Santa to bring? A doll, perhaps? A game?"

"Red, red, red," she said impatiently. "Birthday balloon."

My aide, Rosa, who was working nearby with one of the boys, lifted her head and smiled sadly at me. Carla would be one of those children for whom there would probably be no celebration beyond what we offered at school. She had no father. Her mother's boyfriend had just gone up for seven years in the penitentiary on drug charges. I realized that to Carla even a red balloon might seem an extravagance.

After school Rosa and I discussed the matter. "I'll tuck a balloon in," I said. "I think I have some left over from Nathan's birthday."

"I want her to get a nice present," Rosa said. "Maybe a little doll. Something to play with."

❄ ❄ ❄

On the afternoon of the party, the children were in a frenzy of excitement. At 1:30, Santa arrived, *ho-ho-ho-*ing his way into the gym and dragging an enormous bag full of presents. The children screamed with pleasure and surrounded him.

"This is really going to be good," Rosa whispered.

"I love this. I love seeing their expressions." Sharing her enjoyment, I settled into a chair to watch. First one, then another of the children received their gifts, oohing as they opened them and running over to us to show them off.

"Here comes Carla's," Rosa said, as Santa Claus lifted out a big parcel and put it into Carla's waiting hands. For several moments Carla did nothing but hold it out at arm's length and regard the gift wrapping.

"Look at her," Rosa said with affection. "She's over-whelmed."

Indeed, she appeared to be, so I got up and went over. "What have you got there?" I asked and knelt beside her. "Do you want to open it?"

Hunkering down on the floor, Carla ripped off the wrapping. Inside was a big brown teddy bear. "Oh, what a wonderful present!" I said.

Carla began to cry. "No balloon. No birthday balloon."

"There's a balloon here, sweetheart. Look . . ." I rummaged through the paper to pull out the red balloon we'd included with the bear.

"No." Carla wept. "Birthday balloon go up, up, up."

"I can blow it up. . . ." I began, and then it dawned on me. "A helium balloon? You wanted one that floats?"

She nodded through her tears.

There were thirty-five minutes left to the school day. I turned to Rosa. "Can you keep track of things? I'm going to try to get Carla a helium balloon."

"From where?"

"I don't know. But I'll be back before school lets out." Grabbing the red balloon, I headed out to my car.

I tried the dime store, the drugstore, the card shop, and finally a gas station. Yes, the attendant said, they had helium: $53 for a small bottle, with a $20 deposit to insure that I brought the bottle back.

"I only want to blow up one balloon," I explained.

"Sorry," he said.

"Come on," I pleaded. "It's Christmas." At last he relented and filled the balloon for me. I raced back to school with it, just in time.

Carla's face, when she saw the red balloon, made all my efforts worthwhile. She ran pell-mell across the gymnasium to fling her arms around my waist. I grabbed a discarded piece of ribbon and tied it to the balloon, then handed it to her. "Here you are. Santa forgot to bring this in for you."

Smiling gloriously, she let the balloon float gently upward. "Birthday balloon," she crooned. "Up, up, up."

Then it was time to put on boots and coats, to collect goodies and go home. As I helped the boys get ready, Carla sat on the bench in the cloakroom and played with the balloon, letting it rise, pulling it down, letting it rise again.

"Carla, time to go."

"Carla's dorky," Mikey said. "It's just a balloon."

"It's because she's nothing but a *re*tard," Nathan replied.

I gripped Nathan's collar and spun him around the corner into the classroom to have a few words with him, but Carla still sat, oblivious, and played with her balloon.

After seeing the boys down to their rides, I returned to the cloakroom. "Carla, come on. Your bus is here." I helped her on with her coat. "Here, get your scarf on, too. It's cold out." She watched the balloon bounce as she tugged the ribbon. "Let's go. I'll walk you down."

"Birthday balloon," she was murmuring to herself. "Happy birthday."

Her bus was parked at the far end of the drive, but she didn't hurry. She was holding the balloon in front of her and gazing up. Then, without warning, she let go. The breeze caught it and sailed it upward.

"*Carla!*" I cried in dismay. "*Now* look what's happened!" All that trouble I'd gone to, and she'd simply let the balloon go. I felt like yelling at her, Christmas or not.

But Carla only stood, watching the balloon rise high in the gray December sky. "Up, up, up," she whispered. "Birthday balloon up in sky."

"Yes, it's up in the sky, all right," I muttered gloomily.

"Happy birthday, baby Jesus," she said. "Happy birthday." And she turned to me and smiled.

Torey Hayden

Torey Hayden specializes in children and child psychology. Today she lives and writes in Scotland.

Joseph Leininger Wheeler

POSADA

Was there no escape in this wide world from unrelenting stress? from one work deadline following another, with never a breather in between?

❄ ❄ ❄

*D*okta, this is Jenna."

"As if you had to tell me—no one else calls me 'Dokta.' . . . *So*, how's my goddaughter?"

"Not good at all. I—I need to see you this morning, if you can possibly squeeze me in."

"No problem. Come on down. It's a zoo this morning, but I'll have the receptionist send you right in."

"Thank you. I'll leave my office right away and should be there in about thirty minutes."

❄ ❄ ❄

After a cursory exam, the doctor asked Jenna to follow him to his office and take a seat. The receptionist held all nonemergency phone calls at the doctor's request as he sat down behind his desk and leaned back, fingers clasped behind his head. He paused momentarily before he asked in the most serious tone of voice she'd ever heard him use, "Are you trying to kill yourself?"

"What do you mean?"

"Just this: You're on the brink of a total collapse. What's that ad agency doing to you? Never mind. Knowing your boss so well, I don't even need to ask. Tell me, when was the last time you took a vacation?"

"I can't remember."

"Thought so. How many hours a day do you work, generally?"

"Ten, twelve, fifteen."

"How often?"

"Most days. I *have* to, to keep up."

"Five days a week?"

"No—weekends, too."

"How long has this been going on?"

"A year—two years. I can't remember when it wasn't this way. Every once in a while, I take a weekend off."

There was a long silence as her godfather studied her, deep concern in his eyes. Finally, he pulled out a prescription pad, wrote enough to fill three pages, then handed it to her, saying, "Read it!"

After bemusedly reading it, her feverish eyes widening, she looked up and said, "But I can't. I can't! I'll lose my job!"

"Then *lose* it—better your job than your life!"

"You're joking, aren't you? You can't really mean this."

"My dear woman, I've known you for—what is it—thirty-some years now?"

"Thirty-three . . . and three months."

"Plus nine months in the womb, make it thirty-four." She smiled faintly.

The doctor did not smile. Removing his glasses, he wiped them off, then continued, "Jenna, you've always been disgustingly healthy. But you aren't now. Why didn't you come in to see me sooner?"

"Too busy, I guess."

"My dear Jenna, the human body can stand only so much stress and continuous work before it breaks down. You've lasted much longer than most, thanks to good genes and good diet. But the body demands regular rests. Sabbaths. Doesn't your church tell you about Sabbaths?"

"Y-e-s . . . but lately I've been too busy to go."

The doctor was quiet for a minute. Then dropping his professional manner, he said, "Jenna, it's really hit you hard, hasn't it?"

"Yes."

He sighed and said, "But I guess there's not much we can do about it now. . . . Now that your dad has made other vows."

"No, Dokta, there isn't."

"So there you have it: still grieving over your folks' divorce and nonstop bludgeoning yourself to death with overwork—and that's not all, is it?"

Miserably, she said, "No, you know it isn't."

"Your fiancé's misdeeds surprised everyone. But Bart is being punished enough without any help from you. Hating him only demolishes what's left of your inner peace."

"I just can't help it. Every time I think of him, it's as if a tiger inside me lunges to the full length of its chain!"

Again, her godfather was silent, studying her with his sympathetic eyes. Finally, he said, "Let's see if I can get a clear picture of your condition: Even two years after your parents' divorce, you haven't yet forgiven your father, have you?"

"Certainly *not*! How could I?"

"Nor the proverbial 'other woman' he's now married to?"

"I don't even want to think about her. She broke up our home. If it hadn't been for her, Dad—" She stopped in confusion.

"And the pain of Bart's betrayal is as sharp as ever, isn't it?"

"I will *never* forgive him. Not in a thousand years," Jenna spat out.

"Some of what you're saying, my dear, I attribute to fever, but sadly, the truth is that hatred and a determination not to forgive are gradually killing you, both in body and in spirit." Another long silence. Finally, with an air of bringing the interview to a close, he said, "My prescription stands. It's imperative that you get away from here. Got any money set aside?"

"Oh, yes. Plenty. Because I work and work and never go anywhere."

"Good. Go home and pack. Call a travel agent and get outside the United States, first flight out, regardless of cost. Just be sure you pick a spot close to a big hospital—in case worst comes to worst.

"Don't tell *anyone* where you're going—except for me, your mom, and your dad. Pack light; leave your cell and laptop at home. Take lots of writing paper and pens along—also the study Bible I gave you last Christmas.

"Once you arrive and recuperate after your collapse—"

"My collapse?"

"Yes, that's why I'm sending you out of the country, so you can cut loose from civilization's electronic tentacles. After you recover, *relax*! Don't push it. Travel around from one hotel base. Then just let the thoughts come. You've dammed them up way too long!

"This is serious business, Jenna. So serious that after you leave my office, I'm setting up an appointment with the president of your ad agency. He's an old friend and a good man at heart, but he's a slave driver who's obsessed with money. I will tell him you are very ill and that I've sent you out of the country to an undisclosed destination."

"What if he fires me while I'm gone?"

"He won't. I know him well, and I've postponed this

lecture too long. He's going to be one repentant man before I'm through with him. Who knows, I may have to give him the same prescription: Send him away on a trip with his wife—may save his marriage."

"But Dokta!"

"Don't 'But Dokta' me. This is serious business! *Are you listening?*"

"Yes, Dokta."

"Do you promise—word of honor—to follow the prescription and my directions to the letter? Also to take the medications I've prescribed?"

"Yes, Dokta."

"Good. . . . When you get away from the Dallas treadmill and all the people and projects that are killing you, I have one big favor to ask of you."

"Just ask it."

"I plan to. Open up your Bible, talk to God, and forgive. In all three cases."

"Oh, Dokta, I can't! *I can't!*"

"You must! The consequences of your refusal to forgive are too grim to even consider. Unless you forgive, I'll lose my goddaughter—read that any way you wish."

"Okay, I'll *try* . . . but I don't think—"

"Enough stalling! With that attitude, we'll have lost you for good. . . . One more thing, dear. Do you mind if I pray with you before you go?"

"N-o."

Taking her hand in his, he bowed his head and prayed, "Lord, You know how dear Jenna is to me. . . . I ask, if it be Your will, that You restore her to health and life. Speak to her about forgiveness, about permitting the acid of hatred to drain out of her. Comfort her, forgive her, guide her, bless her, I pray."

The woman's eyes were moist when she reopened them. Rising to her feet, she hugged the man who brought her into the world and said, "Oh, Dokta, bless you! I love you, too! I'll try my best to—to do all you say."

"And you'll write me—I mean e-mail me—from the hotel computer room?"

"Oh, I will!"

"Good. And remember, I'll be praying for you. Every morning, every evening, and in between."

THE FOUR SEASONS, ROOM 615

The last forty-eight hours seem a blur to me. The travel agent was so kind and efficient. I said good-bye to Mom and called Dad—said he'd pay my bills. Canceled every appointment. Dokta must have done his work well: not one call or e-mail from work. On the plane, mercifully, they found an empty bank of seats where I could stretch out, as my head has been spinning and spinning. Dokta's pills helped but also numbed me into a zombielike state. In Mexico City, I staggered some in the international travelers' line. Then, I took an official taxi the short distance to the Four Seasons, and here I am in my room. My travel agent said it's the best, the loveliest, and the most serene hotel in the city.

Now that I'm here, Dokta said to stop taking the antifever and antinausea pills, and to let nature take its course. I feel like a violin with my strings tightened till they're ready to snap—have for a long time. Oh, this bed feels wonderful!

And Jenna spiraled into the darkness of a dreamless sleep.

She slept around the clock. The *No moleste* sign on the door kept the maid from knocking. Midafternoon, she got up just long enough to take a bath and flop back into bed. She didn't wake up until the next day.

When she did wake, fever wilted her, and nausea took away all desire for food.

Late in the afternoon, the ringing phone shattered the silence. "Y-e-s?"

"This is Juan Gutierrez, hotel manager. Your doctor from Texas called and gave instructions. He said you need a long, long rest, and asked that until you get your strength back, we have the maid straighten your room and change your linens, stock your refrigerator with bottled water and juices, and bring you a tray of zwieback and assorted crackers each day, continuing to do so until you feel better. Would that be all right?"

"Y-e-s. Most kind of you."

"Your doctor also said to offer you hot herbal tea. Would you like some now?"

"Yes, thank you."

"Very well, the maid—Maria—will be right up. Call us if we can be of any further assistance."

"I will. Thank you."

❄ ❄ ❄

Day after day, and night after night, the pattern repeated itself: the fever and nausea coming again, receding again; coming again, receding again. Jenna's mind was perpetually dizzy and reeling. Kaleidoscopic images out of her past haunted her, whether she was asleep or awake. With no strength at all, feeling as limp as a wet rag, she had barely enough coherence to answer the brief questions of Maria and Mr. Gutierrez.

THE TURNING POINT

After nine days, mercifully, the nausea left her—but not the fever. Another week passed—and yet another. One ever-so-long night, even after a cool bath, the fever, accompanied by bed-shaking chills, returned with such a vengeance that she wept in pain and frustration. Finally, feeling slept-out, she got up, put on her thick white hotel robe, pulled back the drapes, opened the windows wide, listened to the soothing fountain below, and watched the moon emerge above the courtyard wall. Suddenly, Dokta's warning words came back to her, and she realized that, without God, she might *never* fully recover.

Sinking to her knees, she closed her eyes and leaned her throbbing head against the moonlit windowsill. For the first time in many years, she prayed: "Lord, I've made such a mess of my life. . . . I was once close to You, but I've lost my way. . . . I'm angry at people who've hurt me, refusing to forgive them. Dokta says that if I don't forgive them, You in turn won't be able to forgive *me*— or give me peace. But, Lord, I *don't want* to forgive them—they don't deserve it! Yet deep down, I suspect Dokta's right: that I won't know peace till I do. So show me the way, Lord. I desperately need You in my troubled life. Will You lead me, *please*?" On and on she pleaded, until her reserves were gone. Then she rose, climbed into bed, and dropped into an exhausted sleep.

At 3:18 in the morning, she awoke, her body, hair,

nightgown, pillows, and sheets drenched with sweat. She got up, bathed, put on a fresh nightgown, and lay down on the couch until sleep returned.

✳ ✳ ✳

As day broke, she awoke again. *The fever was gone!* And she was suddenly ravenously hungry. Picking up the phone, she asked room service to bring her a full breakfast.

Afterward, dressing for the first time since arriving at the hotel, Jenna retrieved her study Bible, as well as a tablet and pen, from her suitcase. Bowing her head, she prayed, "Lord, here is Your book. As I read it, will You lead me? speak to me? show me the way?"

Because Dokta had suggested that she read the New Testament first, she started with the Gospel of Matthew. In the sixth chapter she read several verses that jolted her.

Right in the Lord's Prayer appeared these words: "Forgive us our debts, as we also have forgiven our debtors" (verse 12).

Plainly, Jesus felt His listeners needed stronger language yet, for two verses later, He restated the admonition: "If you forgive men when they sin against you, your heavenly Father will also forgive you. But if you do not forgive men their sins, your Father will not forgive your sins" (verses 14-15).

Angrily, she looked up. "But, God, that's just not fair! Certainly You can't condone Dad's walking out on Mom. And their vows were spoken in *Your* name! Doesn't that make You angry? It sure does *me*! And . . . and what Bart did is even worse than *that*—*far* worse!"

Twelve chapters later, Peter sidled up to Jesus and asked what was most likely not a very rhetorical question: "Lord, how many times shall I forgive my brother when he sins against me? Up to seven times?"

Jesus answered, "I tell you, not seven times, but seventy-seven times" (Matthew 18:21-22).

That was followed by another of Jesus' stories, this one about a king's servant who owed his master a vast sum of money, what would be millions of dollars today. Fully aware that the king could throw him and his family into jail, the servant begged for mercy.

Knowing how impossible it was for the servant to repay such a vast sum, the king took mercy on him and forgave the debt. But no sooner had the servant been forgiven then he tracked down a fellow servant who owed him a couple of thousand dollars. Grabbing this man by his throat, he demanded instant payment. Unmoved by his fellow servant's pleas for mercy, he had him arrested and jailed until he could pay the debt in full.

When the king heard about it, he summoned the unforgiving servant and told him that since he, who had received so much mercy, refused to show mercy to others, he must go to prison until the debt was repaid.

And in verse 35 was this further admonition: "This is how my heavenly Father will treat each of you unless you forgive your brother from your heart."

All day long, Jenna slowly and prayerfully read through the Gospel of Matthew, writing down her personal commentary as she went. Early in the evening, for the first time in three weeks, she took the elevator down to the lobby and found her way to the computer room. There she typed out and sent three e-mails. The

first and second ones were to her father and mother.
The third read:

> *Dear Dokta:*
>
> *You were so right: Though nausea assailed me for nine days straight, fever lasted much, much longer. Had all this happened in Dallas, I've little doubt, stirring in worry about falling further behind at work, that I would have cracked.*
>
> *In despair, one feverish night, I surrendered to God. Next morning, the fever was gone! Now I've begun what's likely to be a long healing process. Am reading the New Testament every day. Forgiveness comes hard for me. I must be a hard case: Even though I learn in the Bible that God cannot forgive me unless I forgive others, I just can't, can't!*
>
> *Please keep praying for me.*
>
> *Love,*
> *Jenna*

THE PATIO

The fever had taken its toll: Jenna was now so weak, even walking winded her. She spent half of each day flat on her back in bed. But during the other half, she began the process of living again.

Tired of being cooped up in her room, lovely though it was, she escaped to the hotel's dreamlike patio. Delightful from above, at ground level it was almost Edenic. Birds (both wild and in cages) sang out their joy at another day of life. Flowers, shrubs, and verdant lawns were intersected by walkways radiating out from the blue-tiled fountain, its water forever leaping

skyward before gently cascading down to the pool. So
mesmerizing was the fountain that guests could always
be found near it, absorbing its tranquillity. Off to one
side was a banana tree, complete with a ripening stalk of
the fruit. To experience a garden of such quietude in
the midst of Mexico's megalopolis almost took visitors'
breath away.

As Jenna ever so gradually backed away from the brink,
the Four Seasons patio became her retreat from the
chaotic world outside that she was not yet ready to face.

Every day, she read further in the Bible. Perversely,
though, she continued to search for inconsistencies that
might take her off the hook, might enable her to
achieve inner peace without having to forgive those
who had hurt her most. Unfortunately, her search
proved to be a failure. Almost.

The Gospel of Mark was just as intransigent as
Matthew: "And when you stand praying, if you hold
anything against anyone, forgive him, so that your
Father in heaven may forgive you your sins" (11:25).

Neither did Luke give her much wiggle room:
"Forgive, and you will be forgiven" (6:37).

Only in chapter 17 did she find a verse she might find
useful in achieving some leverage against the toughest
kind of forgiveness: "If he sins against you seven times
in a day, and seven times comes back to you and says,
'I repent,' forgive him" (verse 4).

In her evening prayers that night, she used it, saying,
"Lord, neither Dad nor his new wife nor Bart ever
asked me to forgive them, so I'm assuming I won't have
to unless or until one of them does so."

But hardly had she risen from her knees when an

envelope was slipped under her door. Inside, she found
a FedEx communique from Dokta.

Dear Jenna,

*I'm most pleased to hear you've turned the corner and are
getting better. You won't be experiencing any trouble
with your chief. I hit him hard, so much so that he practically begged for mercy before I was through with him.*

*He and his wife are on an extended cruise (close to
three months) on Silversea. Just received an e-mail from
him. He's rediscovering a lot of things—including his
wife, a good woman, more patient than most. He asked
about you. Appears chagrined to discover that his firm has
degenerated into such a sweatshop.*

*This evening, tired from the day, I'd already crawled
into bed when God "instant-messaged" me. Wish He'd
choose a more convenient hour. Anyhow, He told me to get
out of bed and write you. I think you know why He did
so.*

*I suspect that you're still hedging your bets with God. If
I know you at all, at this very minute you're doing your
best to find a loophole, desperately searching for biblical
legalese that will enable you to escape without forgiving.*

*Give it up! According to the spirit of the law, and
according to the spirit of Christ's life on this earth, there
can be no wiggle room. Unless you forgive—not just one,
not just two, but all three—you will not have peace. Ever.*

It's that simple.

You remain in my prayers day and night.

Love,
Dokta

As she laid the letter down, Jenna furrowed her brow and muttered, "Two against one: foiled again!"

❄ ❄ ❄

Several mornings later, Jenna decided she felt well enough to eat breakfast in the patio café. With her creamy white skin and luxuriant midnight-black hair, she appeared so Latin that the waiter didn't know whether to address her in English or Spanish. He compromised with, "A table for one for the señorita?"

She dimpled and answered, "Yes, for one, por favór."

After leading her to a table, he pulled back a heavy chair, seated her, and asked, "Coffee?"

"Si, señor," she said, delighted to be able to dust off her rusty Spanish. Coffee, juices, fresh fruit, breads, cheeses, pastries, and an omelette later, she sank into a reverie of pure bliss.

After some time, during which waiters surreptitiously watched her admiringly and with no little curiosity (in Latin countries, it's not common for a woman, especially a young attractive one, to travel alone), she awakened out of her trance, signed the tab, walked over to her favorite bench by the fountain, settled down on it, and picked up where she had last left off in 2 Corinthians.

About an hour later, she closed her Bible and looked around with new awareness. Along with her returning strength, her interest in life, places, and people was returning. All those qualities had been cauterized by the frantic pace of the ad agency's daily blitz. For the first time since she'd arrived at the Four Seasons a month before, she was aware of the people around her. Where had they come from? Why were they here? What were their problems, frustrations, and goals? Would she get to know any of them?

Suddenly, out of the blue, came the thought: *the bill!* Mama mia! She'd been here at the Four Seasons for a full month: What must the balance be? High time to have a chat with the general manager.

As she entered his office, the manager stood and graciously welcomed her. "Good morning, Miss Giordano. . . . It's good to see you up. How sad to be all this time in this great city, but not see anything."

"Oh, Mr. Gutierrez, you've been so kind! Everybody has been. Especially Maria, who takes such good care of my room. . . . And yes, this last month has been hard. I've never been this sick before."

"Believe me, we're sorry, too."

"But, sir, the account! I had not even thought of it until now—shows how out of it I've been."

"Oh, yes, Miss Giordano. I'll have an up-to-date copy of it in your hands in just a moment." And he left the room.

Within a couple of minutes he returned with a large mailer. "Here's your account, Miss Giordano. Call me if you have any questions. We look forward to making the rest of your stay here more pleasant than the first." With a smile and a bow, he ushered her to the outer office, saying, "At your service!"

She lost no time in heading to her room. Once there, with trembling fingers, she opened the large mailer. Inside, instead of a bill, was a FedEx packet. And inside it—a letter from Dokta! What could such a letter possibly have to do with her bill?

Since it looked long, she sat down to read it.

Dear Jenna,

Somehow I imagine it will be some time before you're well enough to ask for this. That likelihood has given me time to communicate with several people and make some plans.

What plans? she asked herself.

I've spoken with your chief, your mother, and your father. I pulled no punches as to the seriousness of your condition and the likely results should you remain in Dallas. I read my prescription to each of them.

You should have seen their faces! I told your boss I was prescribing an extended medical leave. He immediately offered to pick up the entire tab for your trip. But I wouldn't let him off that easily: He needs to better understand what it means to micromanage the lives of over two hundred employees. Quite candidly, he is so used to evaluating success by the bottom line that the human factor has been all but ignored.

Your mother, though rarely demonstrative, deep down loves you very much. As she looks back over the last five years, she wishes—oh, how she wishes!—she might live them over. And your father, well, we rebonded—as you know, his divorce and remarriage had driven a wedge into our relationship. Only now does he realize that none of us live alone, each act of our lives has a ripple effect in the lives of those dearest to us. If you could only have seen his face when he realized his part in your collapse, you'd not be finding it so difficult to forgive him.

Before these individual meetings, I had a long tele-phone chat with the general manager of your hotel. I leveled with him as to why I had prescribed such a trip for you. He was most empathetic: asked what he and the Four Seasons could do to help. I told him, and he meta-phorically sharpened his pencil and came up with a figure for an extended stay that was more than fair.

I, being an old bachelor who's never had the joy that comes from children of my own, selfishly wanted to pick up the entire bill myself. After all, I've more money than is good for me. But neither your boss nor your mom nor your dad would hear of it. Each carries so much guilt in the matter that it would have been both cruel and presumptuous of me to turn them down.

So, my dear surrogate daughter (if I may call you that), your tab at the Four Seasons is paid in full for 120 days. If you should leave before then, the unused days are to go into a special Four Seasons account, usable anytime, anywhere in their facilities around the world (that's to keep you from checking out early and trying to return the money—see, I know you well).

If I'm right as to the seriousness of your condition—and I'm usually close to the mark in situations like this—I'm guessing that at least three to four weeks will have passed before you read this. This leaves you three full months before you are to return to work at the agency.

If then.

By that I mean this: You are being given a rare gift— the opportunity (in midpassage) to start all over again, to seriously answer the Three Eternal Questions in life: Who am I? Where have I come from? Where am I going? I strongly suspect that you don't now know the answers to any of them. It's not only possible, but even probable, that you may decide not to return to the agency, but rather make a new start somewhere else. That will be strictly up to you.

Now, your ol' Dokta knows you so well, I'm absolutely certain of your thoughts right now: They can't get away with this! After all, I have my pride. I'll find some way, by hook or crook, to return their money! Am I not right? Well, we're foiling your schemes again: Christmas is coming, about two and a half months into your tour at Four Seasons. Christmas used to mean a great deal to a little girl I was always so partial to. That little girl who'd ask me—way back in July!—"Dokta, how many more days till Twismus?" Perhaps, thanks to this journey of self-discovery in Mexico, it may once again mean a great deal to that long-ago girl. Our Christmas gift to you is both unconditional and unreturnable. Would break our hearts if you tried to return it. Receiving gracefully is an even greater talent than giving, you know.

In closing, if you haven't found yourself at the end of four months, you'd be making an old man wondrously happy if you'd permit me to extend your journey of self-discovery even further.

My prayers continue as you seek to learn the good Lord's will for your life—how you may best serve Him.

Love,
Dokta

P.S. Long ago, you anointed me "Dokta." It's almost as sweet a word as "Dad"—a term I'm too old and too late to ever earn.

❄ ❄ ❄

Never in her life had Jenna cried like this. It was just too much! How well Dokta knew her. Knew that pride was her driving force. Knew that she loved giving but grimly resisted receiving. Knew that only the driver's seat was good enough for her. Knew that she was *driven* to succeed.

Knowing all this, he'd boxed her in, cutting off all her exits.

What a Christmas present! From *all* of them. She took them up one at a time, savoring their names, loving them.

Guilt-ridden Mom. Why? Perhaps because she knew full well she could have kept her husband had she been more receptive to his needs. If only she'd shown more affection, exhibited more love, been less hypercritical and judgmental.

Dad. He'd always been openly affectionate to her. Loving, adoring his daughter. He, too, had wanted to pay the entire amount. Always, Dad would have to live with the fallout from the choices he'd made. Knowing he'd made it impossible for her to ever again "go home for Christmas."

The boss. He wasn't just the Olympian in the top floor suite she rarely saw or spoke to. He, too, was a real person, someone who wanted to do the right thing for his employees, but often did not.

Her godfather. This was all *his* doing. Without him, she shuddered to think what her condition would be now. What really moved her was that, of all of them, he, a nonrelative, understood her best. That lonely man with the loving twinkle in his eyes had not only done all this but was praying continually for her soul's salvation, praying that she would find, in forgiveness . . . peace. If anyone ever deserved the title of "surrogate father," it was he.

It was more emotional overload than her weakened body could handle. More relief, too.

She pulled back the blinds, put the *No moleste* sign on the door, crawled into bed, and slept for twenty-one hours.

GOING OUTSIDE

The next morning, she woke feeling as though she had not a care in the world. She could remain in this lovely place for three more months—*free*! Free to roam at will through the city and countryside. Free to think, read, reflect, grow, without the pressure cooker of nonstop ad deadlines. It was just too good to be true. *I feel like a child again!* she almost sang.

Kneeling by her bed, she prayed, "Oh, Lord, You are too good to me! I don't deserve all this. Please don't give up on me. I do have one small victory to share with You this morning. *I forgive Dad.* Completely, without reservation. . . . I know that's only one down, two to go—but it's one more than I had yesterday. Lead me, Lord, each hour, each day, and help me to find a new life."

✳ ✳ ✳

After breakfast, she walked up to the concierge desk. When her turn came, she said, "I'll be here in Mexico

City for some time yet, and I've never been here before. I'd like to really get to know the city and the region around it. Would you be willing to counsel me?"

"Certainly, miss! First of all, let me get you some booklets on the sites."

"Fine. But I already have the Lonely Planet guide to Mexico."

"An excellent choice. One of the best! Have you studied the section on the city?"

"Not yet. I wanted to talk with you first and get something going—today, if possible."

"Are you with someone, or a group?"

"No. I'm on my own."

"Hmm."

Dimpling, she queried, "Now just what does that 'Hmm' mean?"

"Well, miss, we don't want anything bad to happen to you while you're here with us. We would urge you to be exceedingly careful, especially with public taxis. We'd feel better if you'd permit us to arrange for your transportation—except for public buses, of course. Even so, I must warn you: You're in one of the world's three largest cities—over twenty million people. And not all of them can be trusted."

"So, is it dangerous for me to move about alone?"

"Well, I wish it were not so, but in Mexico a beautiful woman—alone—especially a foreigner, is a tempting target to a certain class of people. Every large city has its underworld, and we have ours."

"So what do you recommend?"

"For starters, Jorge."

"Oh?"

"He's our most requested guide. Bonded by Four Seasons. Many travelers will accept no other, so normally there's quite a wait, but we had a cancellation this morning."

"That's great! Just the two of us?"

"Sometimes yes, sometimes no. Would you be averse to being part of a small group from time to time? Cuts the per-person cost."

"Not at all! I would actually feel *more* comfortable that way."

"Excellent. Give me a minute and I'll check his schedule and call him."

"Certainly. I'll get my camera and be right back."

❄ ❄ ❄

"Miss Giordano, good news! Please follow me outside, and I'll introduce you."

Out in the covered circular driveway stood four people. The first was a distinguished looking middle-aged man of Hispanic descent. The other three appeared to be American tourists like her. They included a man and woman, most likely married, in their sixties; and one tall, good-looking man, about forty years old.

The concierge introduced Jenna to Jorge, then said, "I know you'll take good care of Miss Giordano. She'll be with us for some time and is eager to get to know Mexico in as many dimensions as possible."

"Good morning, Miss Giordano. How special to have you join us. You're from where?"

"Dallas, Texas."

"Oh, another special city. I've a nephew there. I'll let the rest of you introduce yourselves."

"Hi! My name is Albert Wanamaker, and this is my wife, Marji. We're from La Jolla, California, and plan to be here a few weeks, seeing the sights."

"Good morning, I'm Nicholas Fletcher. I hail from Gold Beach, Oregon. I'm here doing research on Latin American ecodevelopment, a field I'm deeply involved in."

Jorge had missed nothing. Taking out a notepad and pen, he addressed Jenna first. "Miss Giordano, would you mind telling us what you'd like to see while you're here?"

"Oh my! That's a tall order. You see, I've never been in Mexico before. I want to be exposed to all aspects of its culture, so I'll be easy to please: I'm starting from almost a blank slate."

"And what about the Wanamakers?"

Marji answered, "Albert and I travel all over the world. In fact, we're rarely home. We've been to the Mexican Riviera and Yucatan, but never to this part of Mexico. We'll try most anything."

"And you, Mr. Fletcher?"

"I've obviously landed in the right crowd. Like Miss Giordano, I'm here for an education—and from what everyone tells me, we've lucked out with the best guide in the city."

"You honor me, but thank you. Not often do I get an opportunity like this. Usually travelers are only here for a day or two, cramming everything into as little time as possible. They leave Mexico and remember only a blur."

After further questions and note taking, Jorge looked

pensively at the group for a moment, then said, "None of you appear to be rushed. Can't remember the last time I've had the luxury of time. You are also all well-traveled and well-educated. So here is my proposal: I shall slow down my usual pace and give you time to really savor each experience, ask questions. I plan to give you a thorough introduction to my beloved country. I will be with you most of the time; when I'm otherwise committed, I'll choose the best substitute I can find. As to how long each of you stays with us, I'll leave that up to you. Is such a plan acceptable?"

The four murmured in agreement.

"Good. Permit me to add that in the Four Seasons you will meet and interact with the elite of this city, Mexico, Latin America, and the world. But most Mexicans are not part of that elite. I have both strains in me: My great grandfather, a Spanish hidalgo who owned a vast estancia [estate], scandalized his family by falling in love with a beautiful servant girl of Aztec ancestry. I am just as proud of her ancestry as I am of his. If you are to really get to know the nonelite, you'll have to be willing to get outside the box. Get to know the have-nots, the *paisanos*, the fascinating indigenous people that make my country such a magical place. You will experience slums, shantytowns. I even suggest rides in Mexican buses—but let me warn you right now, in this country there is no such thing as a bus that is too full!"

He stopped. "How do you feel about that?"

Jenna responded first. "I'm only speaking for me, but I came here to see, not just part of Mexico, but *all* of it."

Murmurs of agreement from the other three.

A big smile appeared on Jorge's face. "Very well,

you're my kind of people. I predict that you'll be learning as much from each other as from me and your other guides—perhaps more. And you'll learn about more than Mexico. You'll learn about life itself.

"Got your walking shoes on? Good. We're going to the closest thing in sight."

CHAPULTEPEC CASTLE

Since Jenna had arrived at night, this was the first chance she had had to see the city. Immediately outside the Four Seasons was Paseo de la Reforma, the city's grandest boulevard. In only minutes the group had passed through the great gates of Chapultepec Park.

"At four square kilometers," observed Jorge, "this is the city's largest park. Today, with the megalopolis constantly expanding, green space is in short supply. We call this park the city's 'lungs,' since it pumps oxygen for this great body of people. Oh, that someone with vision had given us many other parks like this!"

Ahead loomed six great obelisk-like pylons, dazzlingly white.

"Los Niños Héroes," breathed Nicholas.

Jorge came to an immediate stop, looking at Nicholas with new respect. "Yes, these indeed honor 'Los Niños Héroes,' the child heroes of Mexico, but how did you know who they were, never having been here before?"

"One of my four doctoral areas of concentration at Stanford is Latin American history. Of all the nations in Latin America, Mexico fascinates me most. That's why I'm writing my doctoral dissertation on Mexico."

"Aha! A historian among us! I shall have to walk on *huevos* with this group." The others laughed.

"In fact, I'd better find out just what the rest of you know about my country right now. Let me start with you, Jenna. What's your background?"

"Born and raised in Dallas. Majored in English and fine arts at Baylor. Spent two years in Spain as an exchange student and traveled all over Europe. Then I got the advertising bug and studied extensively ways of separating people from their money. That's what I do now—write advertising copy for a big ad agency."

"Thank you. And you . . . Marji?"

"I grew up in Incline Village on Lake Tahoe. At Sacramento State, I majored in social studies. I have my master's in philosophy and met Albert in the university library. He couldn't get away from me, so we married. We have three sons, whom I stayed at home to raise. Now we're grandparents several times over, and we travel. I agree with Augustine: 'The world is a great book—of which they who never stir from home read only a page.'"

"Bravo, Marji! I'll have to remember that quote. Albert?"

"I'm from Placerville, a small once-upon-a-time mining town in the foothills of the Sierras. At Sacramento State, I majored in biology. After we married, I did graduate study in oceanography in a number of universities in the United States and abroad. I've been lucky. Privileged to partner with Jacques Cousteau on a number of projects. Now I've hung up teaching and research in order to write books and explore the world with the light of my life, Marji."

"Nicholas, what else should we know about you?"

"You mean, follow Albert?" Turning toward him,

"Goodness! Now I know why your name sounded familiar. I've read several of your books. What an honor to rub shoulders with one of the world's living legends in oceanography! . . . As for me, not much to add, just that I grew up in Oregon and California."

Jorge said, "Now that we know what each of us brings to the table, it's time to turn to Los Niños Héroes. . . . Any of you remember what happened in 1846?"

"War with the United States?" asked Marji.

"Right. Who can tell me about 'manifest destiny'?"

Nicholas answered, "I can sense where you're heading. It was the belief that the United States was destined to own all the land sea to sea—that God willed it, and anyone who stood in the way would get little sympathy."

"Well put. And poor Mexico stood in the way. Just a few decades before the Mexican-American War, Mexico had gained independence from Spain, and it was still struggling to maintain a stable government and control its vast territory. By 1846, Mexico still controlled all of California, Texas, Arizona, and New Mexico, as well as parts of Colorado, Utah, and Nevada. That was about 40 percent of the land mass of the lower forty-eight states.

"Since Mexico refused to sell its land, war was declared. Oh, there were other pretexts, of course. General Antonio López de Santa Anna's army marched north and overran the Alamo but lost Texas. In 1847, General Winfield Scott and his men landed at Vera Cruz. Santa Anna's army was defeated at Cerro Gordo, and Scott's army, with vastly superior forces, marched

into the Valley of Mexico (this valley) and quickly overran it. Above you, on the heights, was a military academy. According to the story that has come down to us,
on September 13, 1847, six boys, having defended the
heights as long as they could, wrapped themselves in
Mexican flags and leaped to their deaths rather than
surrender to the Americans. These boys were Los Niños
Héroes."

"Kinda makes that stirring Marine march 'From the
Halls of Montezuma to the Shores of Tripoli' lose its
luster, doesn't it," muttered Albert.

"Study the columns. Note their names. Each of the
six boys is christened in the hearts of his country-
men. . . . Well, the end was foreordained, given the
unequal armies. On February 2, 1848, Mexico signed
the Treaty of Guadalupe Hidalgo. The Rio Grande
River became the new border, and all that vast land
west to the Pacific was ceded to the U.S. for fifteen
million dollars. Baja California was rejected as all desert
and absolutely worthless. Otherwise, California would
have doubled its length.

"Friends, every time I visit some of my favorite U.S.
cities—San Francisco, Monterey, Santa Fe, Taos, and
San Antonio I cannot help but think: *I'm home—this city
was once part of Mexico.*

"Now, after studying the six monuments, let's climb
the hill to Chapultepec Castle."

On the way up, in a low aside, Albert said to Nicholas, "History tends to be written by the winners, doesn't
it. More than a bit humbling and enlightening to hear
from the losers' side."

"True, Albert, but time is a great leveler and sometimes redresses grievances generations later."

When they finally reached the castle walls, Marji asked, "When was this built?"

Jorge stopped the group. "This hilltop has been used by Mexico's people for thousands of years: The Toltecs came here, then the Aztecs. The castle itself was constructed in 1785 as a residence for the viceroys of New Spain. After the revolution, in 1843, it was converted into the military academy we spoke about only moments ago. When Maximilian and Carlota arrived here in 1864, they refurbished it and it became the imperial palace. More on them later."

After touring other parts of the castle, the group came to the imperial apartments. Here Jorge stopped. "Now I want you to listen to a story. I can virtually guarantee that in years to come you will have forgotten almost all that I share with you . . . except . . ."

"Except for stories," finished Marji.

"Correct. We don't remember people because of length of time. Look at John F. Kennedy and his so-called Camelot. Not even three years as president before he was assassinated on November 22, 1963. Yet who of you can forget him and his lovely wife, Jacqueline?

"Just so, Maximilian and Carlota are two of the more famous names in history. Why? Perhaps it's because— like the Kennedys, like Alexander, like Cleopatra, like Marilyn Monroe even—they all had the wisdom to die young. Frozen for all time in the beauty of youth.

"But back to this ill-fated pair. Napoléon Bonaparte was dead, and Napoléon III, unequal in every way to his illustrious ancestor, sat uneasily on the French throne.

Since he bobbled every time he meddled in other nations' business in Europe, he turned his attention to the New World. Given that Mexico was having trouble paying its foreign debts, Napoléon got Britain and Spain to invade Mexico with him and squat on its port cities until all the debts had been paid. But all this was just a ruse: What Napoléon *really* wanted was to conquer Mexico and make it into a Catholic empire run by a puppet emperor. Britain and Spain, realizing they'd been duped, pulled out, and Napoléon, to fill the vacuum, shipped in thirty thousand additional French soldiers.

"But he needed a Catholic emperor with stature, preferably one who wouldn't ask too many questions. Who better than Archduke Maximilian, brother to Franz Joseph, emperor of the Austro-Hungarian Empire? Maximilian and his beautiful wife, Princess Charlotte of Belgium, were only too pleased to accept. After all, spare crowns didn't come around every day, and Franz Joseph showed no signs of dying young.

"So the handsome couple arrived in Mexico City on May 28, 1864, Napoléon's forces having conveniently pushed—so they thought—poor outgunned Benito Juárez (president at the time of the invasion) clear across the U.S. border. Charlotte, now known as Carlota, busied herself refurbishing Chapultepec Castle in an imperial manner and orchestrating the construction of Paseo de la Reforma, a takeoff on the Champs-Elysées of Paris. Unfortunately, the happily-ever-after fairy tale—wasn't. A year later, the long U.S. Civil War finally over, Washington looked at Napoléon's shenanigans and was not amused. It demanded that France pull out. Napoléon III not being Napoléon I, his troops

broke speed records pulling out of Mexico. In despera-
tion, Carlota took a ship to Europe and begged
Napoléon III to live up to his word and the pope to step
in. Both turned a deaf ear to her.

"As soon as the French pulled out, former president
Juárez moved south. It didn't take Maximilian long to
realize that his odds of survival weren't good. Had he
fled and been reunited with his wife in Europe,
Maximilian would today be an almost-forgotten foot-
note in history. Instead, he was persuaded to stay—
perhaps just to please mythmakers—and was betrayed
before being shot by a firing squad. In Europe, Carlota
lost her mind. Presto! Another lost Camelot. And their
myth still brings in the tourists. Kennedy's Camelot
lasted two years, eleven months; Maximilian's, two
years, eleven and a half months.

"As for Napoléon, his nation paid a bitter price for his
spinelessness. Next door, Bismarck was chuckling over
Napoléon's abject flight. Three years later, Germany
barreled across the line and left France in shambles."

TWO JOURNEYS

In the coming days, Jenna found herself juggling two
tracks in her mind: the Jorge-led journeys of discovery
into Mexico and the daily study of her Bible. Jorge
wisely split up their visits to Mexico's equivalent of the
Smithsonian, the National Museum of Anthropology. It
took five separate visits.

One evening, at the end of the first week of tours,
she tackled those dreaded questions. *Where did I come
from?* On the surface, she came from two distinctly
different families: the Italian one, warm, loving, openly

affectionate, family-oriented, and in love with life; the other, methodical, scholarly, undemonstrative, isolationist, and Calvinistic with a martyr complex. *No wonder I'm so mixed up,* she concluded.

So who am I? she asked herself. And it was easy to see where her workaholism came from. She could actually hear her mother's words: "Work until you drop. Never take breaks. You can *never* be good enough—not if you live a thousand years!" And God never seemed to smile. But she also saw where the bubbling joie de vivre of her childhood and collegiate years came from. In retrospect, thanks to her father, this had been the happiest time of her life. Anything had seemed possible then, with God as a friend and confidant.

So when, Lord, did I lose my way? It didn't take too long to isolate the very moment when her life turned sour. She'd just made an impulsive mistake that resulted in the loss of quite a bit of money. Her mother had looked at her coldly and said in a biting tone, "It's time you grew up, took life seriously, got a *real* job! The business world would be good for you, disciplining you to churn out products day after day. If you did that, maybe someday you could amount to something, not be a failure like your happy-go-lucky shiftless father!"

Well, it all had made sense at the time. From then on, she'd ceased to respect her father or take his counsel seriously. Several times, she'd noticed his wounded look. *Two against one*, she could hear him thinking. And now she belatedly realized that her father *never* had been shiftless. How gullible she'd been!

And so it had been: *Together, we drove him out, almost forcing him to seek companionship and respect elsewhere. And what have I gained in return? Sales-driven success because of clever ad campaigns. And I haven't even been able to choose my products, they were chosen for me. A number of times, I made a success of products I didn't even believe in. I've sold the mind God gave me—for money, for status. What if my life were over now? What would I have accomplished?* She thought about product after product and found most to be as ephemeral as meringue on a pie. Metaphorically, she kept dredging down through all the layers of hype to some sort of product, program, or cause she could take pride in. Here and there she found them, but they were few.

So, Lord, did I take a wrong turn when I chose advertising as a career? Not at all—for she was sure advertising could be a career to be proud of. How? Easy. By calling your own shots, by choosing products you really believed in, products of quality, products that would better the lives of those who used them.

And now, *Where am I going?* That's what she was here for, why she'd been gifted with four months of unstructured life. Again, her mind returned to that long-ago crossroads. Had she stayed in English and the humanities, would she be happier now than she'd been in advertising? *Not if I had wrecked that too, by the drive-yourself-into-the-ground philosophy.*

So I really have no idea where I'm going. But I do have time to find out. One thing I do know: It's long past time to write Dad a long letter, telling him just how much I owe him, love him, respect him—and that I've forgiven him.

THE LAST DAYS OF TENOCHTITLÁN

On one of their visits to the Museum of Anthropology, Jorge filled them in on the highlights of Aztec history and encouraged them to learn more through the museum's exhibits. Marji and Jenna were especially interested in one on the everyday life of the typical Aztec woman. They spent an hour walking through the exhibit together, talking and laughing as they went. After reuniting with the group, Jorge led the foursome into a quiet meeting room and had them sit down. He cleared his throat and said, "I shall now share with you one of the most compelling stories in history: how Cortés conquered the Aztec empire.

"Hernando Cortés was born in 1485 in Spain. He came to the New World to seek his fortune, for there was no future at home. He had all the qualities that Maximilian lacked: He was a persuasive speaker and a brilliant strategist, admired by his troops as well as enemies.

"On February 18, 1519, Governor Diego Velasquez of Cuba asked Cortés to put together an expedition to conquer Mexico. But Velasquez was a jealous man and quickly regretted giving the command to Cortés.

"The odds against Cortés's success were almost over-whelming: Against millions of Aztecs he had 11 ships (and he burned them, making it do or die), 508 soldiers, 100 sailors, and 16 horses. But he also knew how to make friends among the other peoples of Mexico. His greatest coup was the princess Marina, a hostage awarded him. She knew the Nahuatl language as well as the habits of the Aztec leaders. She became Cortés's tongue, adviser on Indian affairs, tactician, and wife in all but name. With good reason, the Aztecs called Cortés and Marina by one name: Malinche. And Cortés had one more huge advan-tage: According to the Aztec calendar, in 1519 the light-skinned Quetzalcoatl, their god-king, would return from the east to rule his kingdom.

"So it was that when Cortés, leaving a small garrison in Vera Cruz, marched on the Aztec capital of Tenochtitlán, the emperor Montezuma came out to welcome him as Quetzalcoatl and housed Cortés and his men in a palace. By 1519, this Venice-like city, in the middle of a large lake, had over 200,000 residents (over a million in the valley). For half a year, there was an uneasy peace between Montezuma and Cortés. Then Montezuma, suspecting Cortés was not a god after all, turned against him. At about the same time, Pánfilo de Narváez, who'd been sent by Velasquez to relieve Cortés of his command, landed on Mexico's shores. This was the crucial moment of Cortés's life. In short order, he defeated both Montezuma and Narváez. Cortés then rallied his troops, defeated the Aztecs at Otumba, and launched an all-out assault on Tenochtitlán, conquering it street by street, canal by canal, and utterly destroying it, brick by brick. Finally, Cortés was ruler of Mexico, which became the Spanish colony of New Spain.

"But Cortés went on to make mistakes, especially by permitting his men to be unduly cruel in their treatment of conquered peoples. Distrustful of his ambitions, the royal court began to rein him in. In 1547, in Seville, worn out by years of demotions, litigation, and character assassination, Cortés died. Yet love him or hate him, his story will forever be intertwined with Mexico's."

IF I HAVE NOT LOVE

That night, Jenna found it impossible to sleep. Opening her Bible, she was impressed to reread 1 Corinthians 13, and it hit home like nothing else in the New Testament. Especially lines such as: "[Love] is not rude, it is not self-seeking, it is not easily angered, it keeps no record of wrongs" (verse 5).

It was not merely part of the chapter that left her defenses in splinters, but rather the totality of it.

Do I have love? she asked herself over and over.

She had also been studying Christ's life on earth and His daily interactions with men, women, and children. One defining word kept ringing in the long corridors of her mind: *kindness.* Gradually, she was beginning to see that one word as the long-sought answer. In memory, she could hear her mother say, in an angry tone of voice, "You *must* forgive, or Jesus won't forgive you—so just *do it!*"

But that didn't sound at all like the Jesus she was coming to know. For it wasn't that Jesus was unwilling to forgive—but rather, by filling her own body with the boiling acid of hatred, anger, and determination to never forgive, *she* was walling herself off from both people on this earth and the source of all kindness, all love—God!

IN ALAMEDA PARK

They'd spent all day at the pyramids of Teotihuacán, built by the Aztecs centuries before, and Jenna's mind still reeled at their grandeur and austere beauty. She was especially impressed by the Pyramid of the Sun, one of the three largest pyramids ever constructed, exceeded in size only by the Great Pyramid of Cholula (in southern Mexico) and Egypt's Pyramid of Cheops. And they'd also stood in awe before the Pyramid of Quetzalcoatl, the Pyramid of the Moon, and the great Avenue of the Dead.

She was amazed to think that, between AD 450 and 650, 150,000 to 200,000 inhabitants lived in Teotihuacán, one of the most magnificent cities in the world at that time. She could only imagine how dazzling it must have been to look up at those lime-covered pyramids painted in brilliant red against a deep blue sky!

On the drive back to the hotel, Jenna realized how much she'd come to like and appreciate the four people who shared the car with her. Indeed, as the days and weeks had passed, they were strangers no more, but friends she felt she'd known always. Jorge was like a wise and understanding favorite uncle; Albert and Marji, like the adventurous young-at-heart parents she wished she had. She had discovered that she could talk to Marji with an openness her own mother had never permitted. As for Nicholas, he was somewhat like the longed-for brother she never had—and, rather disturbingly, he was becoming something more.

❄ ❄ ❄

Just before reaching the doors being opened for them by the hotel bellmen that evening, Nicholas stopped her and asked, "Are you exhausted from the day?"

"No. I'm feeling stronger now, more like my old self."

"Good. I feel like walking some more, seeing what the city's like at night. I've had several chats with the concierge staff about venturing off on my own and about restaurants that are safe for Anglos like us. It would be great to have company. Al says that Marji just wants to rest up tonight."

"Why not. Let me buzz up to my room for a few minutes. Meet you back here about half past?"

"Great! See you then."

❄ ❄ ❄

After taking a city bus down Paseo de la Reforma, they disembarked near the Alameda, the city's second largest park. After having explored it for about an hour, they found an empty bench, gratefully sat down, and just took in the vibrant life that eddied around them.

Finally, Nicholas smiled and said, "A peso for your thoughts."

Lifting her eyebrows, she responded, "Aren't you the rich gringo!"

"Yep. My ship just came in."

"Where did it dock?"

"Oh, you literalist, you. Anyway, I offered big money for your thoughts."

"True, and at that price, guess I have to deliver. No one's ever offered me more than a penny before."

"Inflation has reared its ugly head. . . . But back to your thoughts."

"Well . . . I've just been thinking how different this is from the U.S."

"How so?"

"The families. I just can't get over them. Mothers, fathers, children, grandparents, uncles, aunts, nieces, nephews—*everyone* . . . all seem to enjoy being with each other. Sweethearts everywhere."

"True. In the U.S. we've all but lost the inter-generational family. But I also can't help feeling sad."

"Sad! Why?"

"Oh, I was thinking of what's happening to the fabric of Mexican culture. The people here are such lovers of life! My mind keeps going back to that village priest who spoke to us several days ago."

"You mean the one who told us of the devastating impact migrant work is having on the rural Mexican family?"

"Yes, how the man of the family heads north to better the finances of his family. Sends money orders back for a time. Returns about once every year or two then leaves, often with his wife pregnant again. Years pass, and children grow up fatherless. Seventy percent of the men are almost never home. Many families break apart. And the fatherless children grow up cold. . . . Losing the *chispa* that makes Mexico, Mexico."

"Chispa? What's that?" Jenna asked.

"Oh, it's untranslatable. Sort of a synthesis of vivacity, love of life, radiance, and so much more!"

There was a long silence, finally broken by Nicholas. "Ahem, speaking of families, tell me about *yours*."

"Well . . . had you asked me a few years ago, I'd have given you a different answer. But, after thirty-five years of marriage, my parents split up. Dad walked out and left Mom all alone. Found someone else—or that some-one else found him. At any rate, there's no longer a home to go to, come Christmas."

"No siblings?"

"Sadly, no. . . . Just me. . . . And you?"

"Guess I'm luckier. Very close-knit family . . . one brother, two sisters. And we love each other dearly."

"And . . . uh . . . are you married?"

"Oh no. I've always said I wouldn't marry until I find someone who completes me. Someone who'll marry for life—not just until hard times come or problems arise. And God has to be central in her life, more central even than me. . . . And you?"

"I'm not married either. Came close, though. Oooh! I can't even think about it without getting angry. No, *angry* is too mild a word!"

"I wouldn't have thought you to be the angry or bitter type—must have been something terrible he did to you."

"It *was*!"

"So what happened? Or is it a deep dark secret?"

"No. It's common knowledge—at least in Dallas."

"Oh?"

"Well . . . it's a long story. I've known Bart since high school. He was always a good friend to me. In recent years, he became more than that. About five years ago, he proposed."

"And you accepted?"

"Yes."

"And?"

"We were to be married October 12—three years ago . . . and uh . . ."

Nicholas waited in silence.

"It was two weeks before our wedding . . . and Dad rang my doorbell early one morning. With a stricken look on his face, he handed me the newspaper. There, his face on the front page, was Bart."

"What had he *done*?"

Instead of answering, she rummaged around in her shoulder bag that also doubled as a purse. Finally, she found a battered-looking news clipping and wordlessly handed it to him.

As he read, his face blanched.

"Have you spoken to him since?"

"*How could I?* . . . I *never* want to see him again!"

A long silence followed.

She looked at him questioningly. "Certainly you don't think I ought to have continued our relationship after *that*!" Her voice was almost a snarl.

"No. It's not that."

"What is it then?"

"Oh, I was just wondering why anyone would keep such a thing in her purse day after day for—what is it . . . *three years* now?"

Sheepishly, she lowered her eyes. "Guess that *would* seem kind of strange."

Nicholas said nothing.

She continued. "He's still in prison. He'll be there until he's an old man."

Nicholas nodded.

Finally, the silence growing awkward, he said, "From your attitude, I'm guessing you haven't forgiven him."

"Of course not! How could *anyone* forgive such a thing!"

"Even God?"

"God? . . . Oh, I guess God would. He'd *have* to, or He wouldn't be God."

Again, he looked at her in silence.

"Nicholas! I don't understand you. Look at how Bart hurt me—wrecked my life!"

"How? . . . I can certainly see that he made a mess of *his* life, but how did he wreck yours?"

"How?" she sputtered, plainly at a loss for words.

"Yes, *how*?"

Silence.

"Jenna . . . you've got my curiosity up. . . . Your dad—have you forgiven him for walking out on your mom?"

"Y-e-s. . . . Since I arrived here in Mexico, I've finally forgiven him."

"And the woman he's married to now?"

She blazed into fury. "Nicholas! Who do you think you are—a grand inquisitor?"

After a moment of silence, he answered, "No . . . just curious. Wanting to know you better. Find out what makes you you."

"And you're disappointed?"

"Well, since you put it that way—yes."

❊ ❊ ❊

That night, Jenna couldn't sleep. Nicholas had taken a jackhammer to the concrete of her mind, shattering her prejudices and pulverizing her precious sense of martyrdom.

The next morning, she descended to the patio early in order to catch Nicholas alone before breakfast.

When he saw her, he stopped and said, "My goodness! What happened to *you*? Did you sleep at all?"

"No."

"It wasn't something I said, I hope."

"Yes, it was. . . . You've messed up my entire brain."

"How so?"

"Well, before last night, I hated my dad's new wife, and I more than hated Bart. And I was rather comfortable—sort of—in those dual hates, because I felt justified."

"And?"

"After our talk last night, I began wondering about my new stepmother. If she truly loves Dad, she can't be all bad. And I've—I've refused to even speak with her. When I phone their number and she answers—I hang up. . . . Last night, I replayed our conversation at Alameda Park forward and backward, over and over, and was not proud of what I said.

"And . . . as for Bart, for the first time I actually felt sorry for him, considered him to be anything but a monster. What a price he's paying for his crime! Whatever remains of his life after he gets out, no one will want to live anywhere near him. He'll be a pariah, a social leper. . . . And about three o'clock in the morning, this thought came: *I wonder what Jesus thinks of Bart. Is he lost for all eternity?*"

"And your conclusion?"

"Oh, Nicholas, that was the worst of it! I just could not imagine Jesus turning His back on *anyone*—even if that person had descended into hell itself, which, in a very real sense, is where Bart went."

"So . . . do you think Jesus would forgive Bart?"

"How could He *not*? If Bart is sincerely repentant, Jesus wouldn't be Jesus unless He welcomed back to the fold His blackest sheep."

"So where does that leave *you*?"

"Where do you *think* it leaves me?" Then, through her sleep-deprived eyes shone a glory not of this earth: "Oh, Nicholas! At 5:29 this morning I forgave *both of them! . . . I am free!*"

A BELL IN DOLORES—AND AFTER

Several days later, Jorge led the four American tourists through another history museum. As they were leaving, Marji, with a puzzled look, said, "Jorge, I've seen so many names, statues, and real-life mannequins that my mind's in a blur. The Spanish influence is everywhere, yet at some point they had to have left. I'm curious, when and how did it happen?"

With a smile, Jorge directed them over to a low wall, on which they found places to sit. He then said, "Our story starts in the small town of Dolores, where a middle-aged priest named Miguel Hidalgo y Costilla went about doing good to his parishioners, helping them learn more efficient farming methods. It was a quiet life, with every indication of remaining that way. But then an event occurred in far-off Spain that rocked Mexico: Napoléon Bonaparte invaded Spain, deposed Ferdinand VII, and replaced him with his brother, Joseph Bonaparte. A Frenchman wore the Spanish crown! Pockets of incipient revolution broke out all across our country. Hidalgo joined one of them. When the authorities found out and sent soldiers to arrest him, instead of fleeing, Hidalgo rang the church bell to summon his parishioners. It was September 16, 1810. The revolution started right there, and Hidalgo led it, with an image of the Virgin of Guadalupe going before them. Hidalgo, not being a military tactician, made mistakes. His forces were defeated, and he was caught, defrocked, and shot.

"But today, Mexicans consider Hidalgo's ringing the Dolores church bell to be the symbol of the beginning of the revolution, thus our September 16 is equivalent to your Fourth of July."

"So what happened *then*, did the revolution collapse?"

"No, another parish priest, José María de Morelos y Pavón, picked up Hidalgo's torch. He called together the Congress of Chilpancingo in 1813. This Congress formed a government, drafted a constitution, and declared independence from Spain. Things might have gone well except that as Napoléon's troops withdrew from Spain in 1814, Ferdinand reclaimed the Spanish throne and sent troops to Mexico. Those soldiers caught up with Congress, whose members were on the run with Morelos. Morelos fought a rear-guard action long enough to enable the government leaders to escape. Then he was captured, defrocked, and shot.

"In 1820, when Constitutionalists in Spain revolted against Ferdinand, Mexico again declared its independence, and soon Mexico became a republic, at least in name."

Picking up on this, Nicholas said, "I'm intrigued by your cryptic line, 'at least in name.' So far, in your lectures, only Hidalgo and Morelos appear to be national heroes. Have you had no great statesmen, equivalent to our Washington or Lincoln?"

"Yes. One."

"Who?"

"Benito Juárez."

"Oh, him—I see his name *everywhere*. Tell us about him."

"Well, he was born in Oaxaca of full-blooded Zapotec Indian parents in 1806. Both parents died when he was only three. He was educated by the church and studied law. He became a Supreme Court advocate and governor of Oaxaca. For years, he struggled with the Mexican government—even had to go into exile once. Finally, though, he became vice president and, in 1861, president.

"Understand, never before in history had Mexico experienced democracy, so even after it became a republic in the 1820s, it didn't know what to do. Between 1833 and 1855, the presidency changed hands an unbelievable thirty-six times, eleven of the changes perpetrated by General Santa Anna."

"Of the Alamo?" asked Marji.

"The very same. The aristocracy and clergy ruled Mexico as a de facto dual monarchy, but without stability. Everyday life became a nightmare.

"Enter Juárez. He instituted reforms that made Mexico a real democracy for the first time. Just when Mexico began to regain stability, Napoléon III threw his monkey wrench into the machinery, and Juárez and his government fled north. Somehow Juárez kept the flame of nationhood alive during the years of French occupation. Then he recaptured his country and was reelected in 1870, defeating Porfirio Diaz. Diaz revolted, and on July 8, 1872, the long years of trauma, sorrow, betrayal, occupation, and revolution finally caught up with Juárez: He died of a massive heart attack. And Diaz began a semi-benevolent dictatorship that lasted over a third of a century."

Jorge stopped, inwardly reflecting on those terrible years of conflict. Then he said, "It has taken a long time for my people to recognize just how much we owe to this simple unpretentious, impeccably honest man, our first indigenous president and the father of democracy. Juárez brought the ship of state through seventeen of the most momentous and turbulent years of our history. Today, he is considered to be Mexico's Lincoln, the nation's greatest national hero. . . . Walk over to the apartments he and his wife lived in when not on the run. . . . Now *there* was a man for the ages!"

BREAK-IN

Later that afternoon, Jenna and Nicholas met for soft drinks on the hotel patio. "Young man, your time has come!" said Jenna.

"How's that?"

"Well, in recent weeks, you've given me the third degree. Now it's your turn."

Grinning ruefully, Nicholas said, "Uh-oh. Now I've got it coming."

"You most certainly *do*. . . . Tell me your story and why your life has been so much easier than mine."

"*Easier?* Not by a long shot. Just . . . different."

"How so?"

"It's a long story, so I'll condense." Pausing, a faraway look came into his eyes. "I'm a preacher's kid, product of growing up in glass houses. You'd have to grow up in one to really understand."

"Glass houses?"

"Yes. You're watched by parishioners day and night. *Have* to be good—whether you like it or not. . . . I was full grown before I became a Christian on the inside. Till then, it was all external."

"Always a history buff?"

"Always. A voracious reader. Books have been my life. I had over a thousand before I graduated from high school. My library's done nothing but grow since.

"As for Mom and Dad, they were passionate about each other when they were young, passionate during my growing-up years, and they remain passionate today. When one has been absent from the other and they first see one another again, the look they exchange is high voltage, even now. I've always coveted that rarity: passion that can last for a lifetime."

"So what's their secret?"

"Good question. . . . Different as they are, they're soul mates, physically, mentally, socially, and spiritu-ally—they revel in each other's company. They remind me of Marius and Cosette of Hugo's *Les Misérables*. Dad has always been in love with Mom's very essence."

"But that life doesn't sound tough—it sounds . . . strangely wonderful."

"I'm coming to that. . . . The years passed; I went to college and got my bachelor's and master's degrees. I taught high school and college. I dated, thinking I'd found 'the one' several times, only to discover that I hadn't. Always, a certain magical ingredient was lack-ing."

"Which is?"

"Kismet: eyes meeting across the proverbial crowded room. It's either there—or it isn't. A number of wonderful women have come into my life, each attractive in so many ways—but not that one. That indefinable magic spark that arcs between two lonely souls and flames into lifelong passion. It's a *rare* commodity. . . . I'm still looking for what I see in my parents' eyes every time I'm with them. But I digress."

"I like your digressions."

"Then the tough thing happened—at Berkeley. I'd completed the coursework for the doctorate, passed my generals, got my thesis statement approved, researched and wrote for four years. The night before my dissertation was to be turned in, I was so excited about finally being done that I took my closest friends out to eat and celebrate. When I returned, my front door was ajar. I *always* lock it. With a deep sense of foreboding, I started taking mental inventory in each room, growing more and more relieved as I moved through the house. Finally . . . my study.

"Even after all these years, I still choke up when I'm fool enough to retell this story. *My dissertation was gone!* Not just it, but all my research: rough drafts, note cards, bibliography cards, cross index, sources most used— *everything!*"

"Oh! So what did you do?"

"I called the police. They couldn't find any clues— not even fingerprints. Didn't surprise me: The kind of person who'd steal a dissertation wouldn't leave fingerprints."

"Suspect anyone?"

"It could have been any number of people. I wouldn't have known where to start."

"But surely your adviser could have backed you up."

"He could have, had he not died from a heart attack several days before the break-in. Truly, troubles rarely come singly."

"So you never found out?"

"Oh, I found out all right! Years later. I kept up on all the dissertations accepted and published. Sure enough, one day *there it was*! Lock, stock, and barrel, submitted by someone who'd been in a number of my graduate classes. Never liked him: shifty-eyed. I figured he'd be another ABD."

"What's *that*?"

"All but dissertation. It's amazing, but most doctoral students never finish. Coursework is a breeze compared to the research grind of writing a piece of truly original doctoral-level research."

"Did you take him to court?"

"With *what* evidence? He had *everything*—computerized research all looks the same. I had precious little in my own handwriting. I'm not making *that* mistake the second time around, believe me. . . . Besides, I'd always believed punishment, generally speaking, is best left to God. There are laws of cause and effect etched into the very fabric of the universe that play out without any volition of the offender, whether he or she believes in them or not."

"In other words, 'what goes around, comes around.'"

"Right: the flip side of the Golden Rule. . . . Several months ago, the man who stole my dissertation was fired. His colleagues discovered plagiarism in a scholarly book published under his name. In academia these days, it's 'publish or perish.' Since he didn't know how to research, he stole someone else's brainchild—again."

"Do you hate him for what he put you through?"

He stopped, silent. "We're back to a familiar subject, aren't we. . . . Wish I could say that I took it like a man, but I didn't. It's humbling to look back and see how consumed with hatred I became after my dissertation was published under someone else's name. My very personality changed."

"Just like mine did."

"It took a buddy to bring me to my senses. He said, 'Nick, I don't like hanging around with you anymore. You're so hateful—it's changed you. You're not the Nick I used to know. That thief also stole the friend I once knew.'

"I was stunned. I told my friend I needed to go somewhere and think. In the days and weeks that followed, I had to go through the same process you went through. Just like you, in the end, the Bible brought me into saner waters. . . . I got my house in order, forgave the poor guy, started all over again, this time at Stanford. Six years later, here I am: writing a dissertation again."

"And your hatred is gone?"

"Yes. As you discovered, in order to forgive, one has to get rid of the hatred first. Now I truly feel sorry for him: Just imagine the stigma that will always shadow him. Worse yet, the knowledge that the PhD credentials on his stationery, business cards, and books are not his at all, but *stolen*! I'd far rather be me. At least what I've written is my own—and God's. His are the wells I draw from when I create."

"I can't get over the fact that you didn't just call it quits. Instead, you picked up the pieces of your life and started all over again. Nick, I'd guess your parents must be very proud of you."

"Well, they seem to be," looking at her quizzically. "But I do know one thing *I'm* proud of."

"What's that?"

"I've finally graduated to 'Nick.'"

Blushing and in a hurry to change the subject, Jenna said, "If you don't mind, explain to me how you can research at Stanford, teach somewhere, be into eco-development, *and* live in Gold Beach?"

Laughing, Nick responded, "Guess those pieces don't fit together very well, do they? But, just like yours, my life is a vast mosaic of apparently unlike pieces, and only God knows how they'll all fit together."

"I like that metaphor. It's somehow rather comforting."

"It is to me, too. Let's start with the Oregon coast. I was five when Dad was called to pastor a Gold Beach church. Serendipitously, he didn't move again until I was twelve. Broke my heart to leave. But he never sold the house: He and my mom plan to retire there someday. At any rate, at the very core of my being are the sights, sounds, and smells of the beach. The restless gulls, zigzagging sandpipers, corn roasted in driftwood fires, fog banks swallowing up the blue of the sky, heart-stopping sunsets, daily walks on the beach, and—the icing on the cake—the ever-changing Rogue River.

"So, after I grew up and got a job, I put money aside for a piece of land overlooking both the river and the sea. It took awhile since the cost of beachfront property's generally out of sight to all but the rich. Eventually, I lucked out on a bank foreclosure. It's my

Shangri-la. I don't live there yet, but I walk up to it every day when I'm in town. I rent the folks' house from them—right next to a one-of-a-kind used bookstore."

"What's keeping you from building a home there?"

"Finding the dream woman who'll help plan it with me."

"Oh."

* * *

Nicholas cleared his throat. "Moving on, as time passed, I did more and more writing."

"What kind?"

"Oh, for magazines, newspapers, and in books . . . about history, biography, life, travel, ecology."

"So we're finally getting to ecodevelopment?"

"Yes. Years ago I became convinced that, with global population exploding, the planet was doomed unless people came up with ways to save the earth from the people who live on it."

"How?"

"For example, the Oregon coast has to be one of the most beautiful stretches of beach in the world. However, developers up and down the coast are doing their best to wreck it."

"But aren't you one of them?"

"With a difference. I seek ways to preserve that ever-so-fragile beauty for posterity—yet still provide pockets of serenity for those who wish to either live on, or see, the coast. . . . Remember the friend who saved me from hatred?"

"Yes. What a friend he must be!"

"That he is. For years now, he's been riding the lead wave in ecotourism, the coming thing. In fact, he's become the leading ecodevelopment voice in the world and today is a billionaire. Because I have long shared his philosophy and head his foundation, he's made me partner."

"So you don't teach anymore."

"No, I don't. I miss the students and classroom, but I felt the tide of my life ebbing away from the classroom some time ago, and in rushed the tide of writing, research, travel, and ecodevelopment."

"But you're still going to complete the dissertation?"

"Of course!" he said, looking at her in surprise. "Why shouldn't I? As Tennyson put it in *Ulysses*, all life is growth. When growth ceases, you might as well call it quits. I plan to grow until that last breath, when God calls me home to eternal opportunities for growth. And there *are* pragmatic reasons for completing it. Though the PhD doesn't necessarily make you smarter, people *assume* it does, and thus it validates all you say and do once you have it—proof that perception trumps reality."

"You're right. I've sometimes clammed up in the presence of a person with a doctorate, perhaps feeling that anything I might say would pale in comparison."

"My point exactly. You may perhaps be interested in another reason I'm here in Mexico right now."

"Which is?"

"You've heard Jorge refer to Mexico's tragic ecology."

"Yes. Terribly sad!"

"Places like the legendary Copper Canyon, which is vast and deep enough to swallow up five Grand Canyons, have been deforested close to the point of no return. There's also the wholesale destruction of the Chiapas region rain forest and the tragic development of the Mexican Riviera. Well, my partner and I have been able to purchase the largest undeveloped tract of seacoast land in all Mexico, which lies between Oaxaca and Guatemala. After I leave Mexico City, I'll spend several months there developing a master plan that will preserve the coast in perpetuity. It will also enable the native Indians who live there to retain their way of life and dignity, and to create resorts that barely leave a mark on the land. Four Seasons is very interested in partnering with us. If it happens—or even if it doesn't—I'd like to lure Jorge down there to lead out in what he does so well."

INTERMEZZO

Early in December, Jenna began looking forward to Christmas in Mexico. Since the city's Christmas season was so different from what she was used to, she asked Jorge about it.

Jorge said, "You'll note that we observe a very different season than you do up north. Children look forward all year to El Dia de los Reyes, or the Day of the Wise Men, on January 6. The night before, they leave their cleaned and polished shoes out for the Wise Men to fill."

"But, Jorge, I'm even more interested," said Jenna, "in another Mexican Christmas tradition that I've heard referred to, but know little about, starting, I believe, about mid-December."

"Oh, you're referring to *Las Posadas*!"

"That's it! Can we experience this tradition?"

"Sadly, no. We're too sophisticated for these celebrations in the city. Let me do some research, however, and I'll get back to you."

❄ ❄ ❄

Later that evening, as the group left Mexico City's splendid marble opera house, Palacio de Bellas Artes, Nick whispered in Jenna's ear, "How about taking the long way back—via Alameda?"

"Oh, I'd love it!" she said, her eyes sparkling.

They sat on a bench in the park and watched the parade of families stream by. Nicholas bought her a monstrosity of a balloon.

She said, after a time, "My mind is dizzy after almost two hours of the Ballet Folklorico. I've seen a number of other ballets, but never anything to compare with this! The entire history of Mexico portrayed in dramatic color, in music, in dance—my feet just can't stop dancing!"

"That's why I didn't want to go in yet. I needed to debrief with someone—and you were the closest victim."

Smiling roguishly, she said, "I'm at your service, sir." Her heart fluttered. Then, feeling herself on dangerous ground, she said, "And I loved the gondolas in the canals of Xochimilco last night. Jorge seems to be saving the brightest fireworks for the very last. But it was a bit sad."

"Why? I thought it was lively—all that mariachi music!"

"Oh, I don't mean *that*. I'm thinking back to how it once was in the ancient city of Tenochtitlán, with its great lake Venice-like canals, bridges, and causeways— and comparing it to the sluggish waterway that's left."

"I see your point. Did you like Venice?"

"One of my all-time favorite places! I want to go back!"

"That might happen—someday," he observed enigmatically.

Again, she changed the subject. "I wonder if Jorge will tell us about Las Posadas? I'd so much love to see the celebration before I—oh, I hate to even say it!— *leave*."

"Me, too—a magical part of my life is coming to a close."

TAXCO

On December 12, Jorge led them into the quietest part of the Four Seasons lobby and invited them to sit down. After clearing his throat, he said, "For the first time since I started leading tour groups, I'm truly satisfied. We've seen not only the city, but the outlying districts as well. Museums, art galleries, churches—we've done them all. In fact, you now know Mexico better than most Mexicans. I've reached the end of what I can teach you—almost.

"The 'almost' has to do with Jenna's desire to experience Las Posadas: Mexico's greatest gift to the Christmas season. How would you like to spend the nine days of

Las Posadas in one of Mexico's loveliest towns, the colonial silver city of Taxco?"

"The very thing!"

"Why not?"

"When do we go?"

"I gather you approve," said Jorge, relieved. "I took the liberty of tentatively booking you in Hotel de la Borda. Not because it's the newest or most luxurious— but because it overlooks the town, has been beloved for so many years, and because of its history and who it's named for."

"Are you deserting us?"

"Not at all. My brother Pablo lives in Taxco. When I called him two nights ago, I told him about you, my adopted family, and your desire to see Las Posadas. Immediately, he invited my wife, Carlota, and me to spend the Christmas season with his family. Last night Pablo, who manages de la Borda, called me with some incredibly good—and I'll confess, totally unexpected— news. Ordinarily, Las Posadas is limited to a select group of townspeople, but since Pablo and his wife, Marta, are one of the nine participating households, and since both of our families are to participate during the nine nights (all in costumes of the time of Christ), he secured permission for you to join us in the procession as well."

"Bravo!" trumpeted Nicholas.

"Additionally, on the final and most important night of all, *La Noche Buena*, December 24, the procession will conclude Las Posadas at Hotel de la Borda."

"Wonderful!" exclaimed Jenna.

"So, for the next three days, you're free to wander around the city on your own. See you on December 15 at 9:00 a.m., our usual spot. I'm taking a van to accommodate the extra luggage and give you more room to spread out. *Hasta entonces.*"

✳ ✳ ✳

On December 15, with everyone unpacked in Taxco and fittings for the Posada costumes made, Jorge gathered them together on the broad patio deck of de la Borda and said, "Before we get to Las Posadas, let me tell you a little about this, one of my favorite towns in all of Mexico.

"Originally, it was called Tlachco—'the place where ball is played'—by the Aztecs. In 1529, the city itself was founded by Captain Rodrigo de Castañeda, who had been ordered to do so by Cortés. In 1531, the first Spanish mine on the North American continent was established here. Originally, they dug for tin, but soon discovered tremendous lodes of silver. But, after they mined it out, the town went back to sleep.

"Two centuries later, in 1743, Don José de la Borda, who had emigrated here from France in 1716, was riding his horse near where the cathedral Santa Prisca now stands. His horse stumbled, dislodging a stone. Dismounting to check his animal's leg, de la Borda discovered silver beneath the stone. De la Borda went on to make three fortunes from that silver, and spent two of them. Unlike most employers of his time, he treated his miners with kindness and respect.

"Right where his horse tripped, de la Borda decided to thank the God who caused the stumble by constructing an elaborate church dedicated to Santa Prisca. You know her as Priscilla, wife of Aquila. Both were influential early church leaders who knew the apostle Paul well. The local Catholic hierarchy permitted de la Borda to donate the church to Taxco on the condition that he mortgage his mansion and other assets in order to guarantee its completion. It was designed by the Spanish architects Diego Duran and Juan Caballero, and de la Borda came close to being bankrupted a third time by its cost. The sculpted altarpiece is covered with gold. But de la Borda smiled as he paid the bills, saying 'Dios da a Borda, Borda da a Dios.' Anyone know what that means?"

"God gives to Borda, Borda gives to God?" answered Jenna.

"Correct. We will get to attend midnight mass in Santa Prisca on Christmas Eve. As for the city itself, unlike many colonial cities, it has not been wrecked by encroaching industrial suburbs. The federal government has declared Taxco to be a national historic monument, and local laws preserve its colonial architecture and heritage.

"Drink it in and be thankful that, after almost five hundred years, this gem of architectural beauty is still with us. Now, what do you say to going in for dinner?"

LAS POSADAS

The next afternoon on the patio terrace, Jorge said, "Now let me tell you about Las Posadas. Perhaps you have noticed that in Mexico a crèche or nativity scene, not a Christmas tree, rules supreme as the focal center of family life during the entire Christmas season.

"By extension the tradition called Las Posadas was

born somewhere in rural Mexico. On each evening between December 16 and December 24, the townspeople reenact Mary and Joseph's difficult search for lodging after their arduous journey to Bethlehem.

"In towns where Las Posadas is held, children's thoughts in early December center increasingly on the coming nine nights. They wonder: Who will get to be the Virgin Mary? Who will get to be Joseph? Who will get to be the hard-hearted innkeeper when Mary and Joseph seek *posada* (a place to rest for the night), and who will at last get to welcome them in? Every time children pass a crèche, their thoughts turn to that dramatic reenactment only days away.

"Finally, December 16 arrives, and nine families choreograph the activities. Starring roles are assigned to children, and the other people are arbitrarily separated into two groups: the cruel innkeepers and the holy pilgrims. Each pilgrim is handed a lighted candle, and a procession is formed, with an angel leading the way, followed by Mary, Joseph, and the pilgrims.

"The long journey from Nazareth to Bethlehem is spread out over the nine nights. As you will see, once the procession starts, all else in the life of Taxco will seem to stop while the two-thousand-year-old drama is played out. Carrying his staff, Joseph will lead a donkey. On the donkey's plump back is the most precious thing in the universe: little Mary, who carries within her the Savior of the world. We will accompany the friends and relatives who surround them. The mood on the streets will be set by candlelight and sacred music. The procession will stop at nine houses. At each door, Joseph will plead for posada; at each door, he will be unceremoniously turned away. Finally, at the ninth house, the door will be opened wide, all of us will be welcomed in, and all will sing thanks.

"For nine consecutive nights, the pageant will be repeated, for on each night, posada is offered at a different home, though each evening will end at the home designated to be the stop on the ninth night. There, blindfolded children will take turns swinging at piñatas—followed by the scramble for the shower of fruits, gifts, and candy when one finally breaks."

"And how will the last night be different?" asked Jenna.

"Oh, *La Noche Buena* will be extra special, the most lavish of all, and the place chosen has to be large enough to hold perhaps hundreds of people. The altar will be decorated with tinsel and flowers, and the infant Jesus will be placed in a moss-lined crib. The whole party will sing many more songs. Then there'll be foods, sweets, liqueurs, and dancing until it's time to go to Santa Prisca's just before midnight.

"Just wait until you hear the bells of Santa Prisca welcome Christmas!"

❄ ❄ ❄

And so it began. Every day they explored the city and the surrounding region; every night they joined in the procession. Since the Americans' once-rusty Spanish had become considerably less so since arriving in Mexico, the children shyly and rather quickly took them into their hearts. Many of the adults became their friends as well. Each night, it was like stepping backwards into time for, in that candlelit procession, the modern world ceased to exist. Instead, the shuffling of hundreds of feet, the donkey's *clip-clop*ping on ancient streets, the swaying Mary and solicitous Joseph, the *rat-atat-tat* knocking at each door, the refusals of Joseph's requests for lodging, the haunting beauty of their singing, and the warm welcome awaiting them at the ninth house—well, without realizing it, each North American pilgrim was changing inside, each in a different way.

Suddenly, it was over. Since they slept in after being up until almost two on Christmas Eve, it was the afternoon of Christmas Day before the foursome began to emerge from their rooms.

Nicholas, after an extensive search of the premises, finally found Marji leaning against a parapet, so lost in reverie that he waited in silence rather than speaking. Finally, sensing his presence, she turned and smiled.

"No place in all the world quite like it, is there?" he said.

"No, there isn't. It may seem silly, but I've been time traveling, imagining myself in this legendary city two hundred years ago. It was not hard—for little has changed. Almost closing my eyes, I envisioned a city of men on horseback, hidalgo women in sumptuous carriages pulled by thoroughbred horses, native Mexicans hawking their wares on the streets, bougainvillea enflaming balcony after balcony, birds everywhere, and there right where it is today, recently constructed Santa Prisca, dazzling in its newness. I—I needed this serenity—the all-intrusiveness of the electronic age back home has been smothering my soul! . . . Guess I'd better come out of my time warp." She sighed.

After a companionable silence, Nicholas cleared his throat and said, "Mother Marji—" so much had he come to admire her that, for some time now, he'd called her Mother—"can I bend your ear?"

"Of course. Come on in—we won't be disturbed here. What is it?"

"I'm in turmoil. Tomorrow, we go our separate ways—and . . ."

"And you don't know where you stand with Jenna?"

"How did *you* know?"

"I've known you were in love since the first time you set eyes on her."

"Have I been *that* obvious?"

"Only to a mother. God gives us a sixth sense for relationships. Let me grandfather Al in, too, as it didn't take him very long before he remarked to me, 'I think Nicholas has got it bad.'"

"Oh my! And I thought I was keeping the secret to myself."

"Don't take it so hard, Nick. There are worse things than being in love."

"Even loving—but not being loved back?"

"Do you know that for sure?"

"Well, every time I try to steer a conversation toward the personal, she adroitly changes the topic on me— *every last time.*"

"That may not mean what you think it means. Al and I feel she cares about you—a lot."

"But I want more than 'a lot.' I want all of her. I want to marry her and spend the rest of my life loving her, just as my father has with my mother."

"Nick, you're aware that Jenna and I have become close?"

"Yes. I can see she adores you."

"Uh . . . excuse me as I do a little thinking. I want to make sure I don't divulge anything intended to be strictly confidential."

Nicholas waited.

"I know she's told you about the breakup of her folks' marriage and the terrible revelation that stopped her marriage to an unworthy man."

"Yes, she has."

"So you're fully aware that she's a deeply wounded dove. She told me several days ago, 'I don't think I'll *ever* marry. If my folks' marriage could collapse after all those years . . . and if someone I'd known so long could turn out to be so different from what I assumed him to be . . . what earthly chance do I have to find someone who'll love me for life—even after I get old and lose what looks I have?'"

"And you told her?"

"That would be privileged information. . . . But I did tell her not to be so quick to rule out the possibility of great happiness with someone different. . . . And I firmly believe, if she could ever put all this behind her, she'd be the most loving wife a man could ever dream of. . . . Nick, if I didn't really believe that you two were made for each other, I wouldn't be prolonging this conversation."

"Mother Marji, what do you think she wants to do with the rest of her life?"

A long silence followed by, "On the surface, just keep running."

"And deep down?"

"Deep down, she wants to find a mate who'll consider her to be his all in all, whose eyes will light up every time she comes into the room, who'll be her best friend and confidant, who'll make her a partner in his life's involvements, who'll keep God central in the relationship . . . and who'll be a loving and constant father to her children. Deep down, she's a whither-thou-goest woman."

"That's what I assumed her to be. But I've been disappointed, disillusioned, and just plain wrong so many times, I've come to doubt my own judgment. . . . And time's running out. If I can't break through before she leaves, I don't feel she'll ever give me another chance."

"I think you're on target there. In fact, last night she told me, 'It's time for me to go. I'll be leaving Taxco the day after tomorrow.'"

"Did she say where she'd be going?"

"No. I don't think she wants anyone to know—so you've not a moment to lose!"

"Oh, Mother Marji, the last nine nights have been awful. In the Posada crowds, she was so near to me, yet so far! She really got caught up in the drama, feeling she was *there*. And I'd look at her, so beautiful in that long-ago robe, and say to myself, *If you won't be mine, the sun will go out of my life!*"

"Only a bold stroke can change her mind—That's it! *That's it! That's your only real chance!*"

"*What's* my only chance?"

"Are you game to be part of a drama for two and follow my script to the letter?"

"Huh? Well, I guess so. Just show me the lines."

❄ ❄ ❄

The shadows of evening dropped down over the Silver City of Taxco. Nicholas stood outside the entryway little Joseph had knocked at the night before. He knocked nine times: *Rat-atat-tat! Rat-atat-tat! Rat-atat-tat.*

Moments later, Jenna opened the door. "Why, Nick!" she said, with a smile of pleasure. "Come on in! And Marji said she'd meet us here. She should be joining us any minute."

Her ever-so-near loveliness almost destroyed his plan of action, but he regained his composure just in time, for she was beginning to look at him quizzically. He said, with a pleading note in his voice, "You've taken part in dramatic productions, I know. Well, I have a favor to ask on this Christmas Day: I'd like you to participate in this impromptu play."

She smiled. "You're funny and unpredictable as always. What are my lines?"

"Just improvise. . . . Listen!" and he changed his tone, saying in a weary voice, "Oh fair maiden, this is my ninth night, seeking posada."

She remained properly stern. "Have you come far?"

"Very far—even from a far country."

"That's not in the script: You're from Bethlehem. You're flubbing your lines."

"I'm improvising too. Play along with me, please."

"Well," she said with a sigh, "all right. Go ahead."

"I'm from a far country, and this is the ninth door I've knocked at—all the rest have turned me away."

"They turned *us* away, Nick!"

"No, this time it's *me*. In Las Posadas, when I knock at the ninth door, what do they have to do?"

"Nick, you're impossible! You know as well as I do that they open the door, welcome you in, and treat you as one of the family."

"Do they—I mean you—*have* to do that?"

"Of *course*! Didn't you learn *anything* during the last nine days?"

"Yes. I learned a lot!"

"Couldn't prove it by me!" she said, her lips primly set.

Now Nick reverted back to the Nick of old. As he spoke, she could no longer question where the action of the play was heading. At first, she looked at him as though he'd lost his mind before it finally dawned on her what he was doing. As he spoke lines not in his script and looked down at her, the light of awareness began to glimmer in her eyes, followed by a growing radiance and lips that twitched.

"This is my ninth night, and this is my ninth door," Nicholas said. "I am asking for posada, and tradition dictates that you welcome me in. But I want you to know that I ask not just for this night, but rather for all time! For I want to marry you and love you always! From the very first day I saw you, walking toward us under the hotel portico, my heart melted, and I knew I'd found what I'd searched for all my life: the soul mate my father found in my—"

Heaven was in her eyes, as she gently placed her fingers on his lips and said, in a voice that was a wondrous mixture of paean, lecture, chuckle, and rapture: "Hush, dearest Nick. Sometimes you talk too much."

Then she was in his arms—and neither spoke at all.

✳ ✳ ✳

Off to the side, three people surreptitiously took in the tableau and quietly retreated once they saw that Nick clearly needed no help from *them*.

In a moment, Albert said, in a voice as deadpan as if he were quoting stock-market figures: "The Four Seasons courtyard will be just right for the pre-wedding reception."

Jorge said, "This is what I envision: It is night, and I see many candles. Oh! It's practically the whole town of Taxco, all those who dressed as pilgrims and innkeepers in Las Posadas. Half accompany one horse and carriage, and half accompany the other—Mexicans *love* romantic stories—especially those set in Mexico."

And Marji, hardly able to contain her joy, added, "And I see the great doors of Santa Prisca opening, and in comes the loveliest bride in all Mexico, in a traditional Spanish gown with a long train. Up in front a tall, handsome man takes it all in: sees the girl who was Mary coming down the aisle, dropping flower petals as she goes—followed by sober little Joseph, carrying the Bible on a cushion. And then comes a dreamlike vision in white, ushered down the long aisle by her father."

"But," said Jorge, getting in the last word, "it was the ninth knock on the ninth door that did it."

HOW THIS STORY CAME TO BE

For a full year, I prayed that God would gift me with a very special fifteenth anniversary Christmas story—but it didn't come. Finally, when I had only four weeks left, I prayed about it almost continually.

Then came our family's trip to Mexico City to see my brother Romayne perform a piano concert on the great Zocalo square. He lives on the rim of Mexico's beautiful Copper Canyon. While in the city, we stayed at the Four Seasons on Paseo de la Reforma. As for Taxco, some years ago, we were privileged to spend Christmas there in the de la Borda Hotel. And on Christmas Eve, singing as they came, the entire Posada procession entered the hotel: the ninth door of the ninth night.

Upon returning home from our latest visit to Mexico, a Voice said, *You have the setting. Now write it.* So I did, all the way to Payson, Arizona, on a lapboard, while my wife, Connie, drove. I wrote that same way on the return from the five-day trip, and all the next week at home.

A number of times I was so discouraged, I almost quit, for the story refused to permit itself to be condensed. Yet each of its many pieces proved essential to the playing out of the plot.

Through no volition of my own, I was strongly impressed that the theme "Those who refuse to forgive others cannot be forgiven by God" had to be the very core of the story.

Are you a Joe Wheeler fan? Do you like curling up with a good story? Try these other Joe Wheeler books that will give you that "warm all over" feeling.

HEART TO HEART STORIES FOR MOMS

This heartwarming collection includes stories about the selfless love of mothers, stepmothers, surrogate mothers, and mentors. Moms in all stages of life will cherish stories that parallel their own, those demonstrating the bond between child, mother, and grandmother. A collection to cherish for years to come.

CHRISTMAS IN MY HEART
Volume XIII

Because the Christmas season too easily becomes a hectic race of *doing*, we often forget to stop and celebrate the greatest gift of all. In *Christmas in My Heart, Volume 13*, enjoy looking over someone else's to-do list; meeting a young boy with a heart for orphans; and watching a soldier yearn for a love that might have been. Stories simply told, but full of wonder.

CHRISTMAS IN MY HEART
Volume XIV

Amid the many joyful traditions of the Christmas season, people sometimes experience difficulty— losing a loved one, an uncertain job situation, or even the anxiety of a hectic Christmas schedule. In the heartwarming stories of *Christmas in My Heart, Volume 14,* you'll celebrate love's triumph over brokenness and rediscover the joy that awaits you at Christmastime.